ALSO BY ANNE RENWICK

ELEMENTAL STEAMPUNK CHRONICLES

The Golden Spider

The Silver Skull

The Iron Fin

Venomous Secrets

ELEMENTAL STEAMPUNK TALES

A Trace of Copper

In Pursuit of Dragons

A Reflection of Shadows

A Snowflake at Midnight

A Ghost in Amber

ELEMENTAL STEAMPUNK STORIES

The Tin Rose

Kraken and Canals

Rust and Steam

A GHOST IN AMBER

AN ELEMENTAL STEAMPUNK TALE

ANNE RENWICK

www.annerenwick.com

Publisher's Note: This is a work of fiction. Names, characters, places, and incidents are a product of the author's imagination. Locales and public names are sometimes used for atmospheric purposes. Any resemblance to actual people, living or dead, or to businesses, companies, events, institutions, or locales is completely coincidental.

A Ghost in Amber/ Anne Renwick. — 1st ed.

ISBN 978-1-948359-34-4

Cover design by James T. Egan of Bookfly Design.

Edited by Sandra Sookoo.

To my developmental biology professor who lectured on the genetics behind dextral and sinistral snail shell curling and planted the seeds for this story many, many years ago.

And to whomever who decided snail slime was the perfect ingredient for facials.

THANK YOU TO...

My husband for suggesting Halloween.

Dr. Patricia Pugh of Emergency Medicine for taking time out of her busy day to answer all my strange questions about septic shock and point me in a better direction. Any errors are my own.

Sandra Sookoo, my brilliant editor who mercilessly ferrets out weaknesses and sets my work on a better course.

My two boys.

My mom and dad who made reading and science priorities.

Mr. Fox and his red pen.

CHAPTER ONE

Somerset, England
October 31, 1885

"CANCELLED?" With a single word, weeks of preparation snapped like a copper telegraph wire subjected to an unexpected gale. "On such short notice? What of the houseguests, the extensive preparations?"

A current of anticipatory excitement had electrified Lady Diana Starr ever since the invitation to the event arrived in the post. But now, with a pop and a fizz, her energy drained away. To be so close, three miles from the chance of a lifetime, yet denied access?

Her mind rebelled. Absolutely not. There must be some mistake. Spending the evening in this ancient, soot-stained pub listening to increasingly intoxicated locals swap ghost stories was not in her plans.

Tonight was the night. The mysteries of Batcote Hall beckoned, and Diana would not be deterred. In that musty old house, a dead man's field notes moldered upon shelves, his collections crumbling in collapsing cardboard boxes. All of it covered in strata of dust, begging to be liberated and dragged into the light of day.

While others danced the night away, she'd meant to slip into the library. Were she so fortunate as to pinpoint the location of the long-lost treasure, a quick inventory to assess its zoological value would have been in order. With a firm grasp of the materials in hand, she'd planned to approach the current Lord of the Manor to make an impassioned presentation, to detail the reasons he ought to grant her exclusive rights to assemble a catalog of his uncle's collection whilst publishing a series of groundbreaking monographs.

But their hired carriage had not arrived, stranding them upon flagstones of blue-gray Wilmcote Limestone before their inn. As ladies did not proceed to a ball on foot, no matter the location, they'd retreated indoors, to the pub, where gossip had informed them of a misfortune of grand proportions.

Diana slid a hand over the silver spangles sewn onto the satin of her midnight-sky gown. Her fingers worried the bright punched metal circles that formed the Pleiades, the seven sisters. Nearby, Orion took aim. It was All Hallows' Eve, and she was the night sky. A disguise to satisfy a mother intent upon securing her daughter a husband, a sister insisting upon one last appearance as a paired set, and her own requirements: slipping into shadows unnoticed.

A gentleman wearing a Tudor-styled doublet, hose and a fur-edged cape answered. "I'm afraid our would-be host,

Lord Wraxall, is bedridden." He answered Diana's question, but directed the entirety of his fawning attention at her sister, Aurora, garbed as she was in a golden gown studded with beads of amber.

Easy to overlook the stars and the moon when the bright morning sun's rays cast them into the shadows with the coming of dawn.

But Diana had come to prefer the dark recesses. There was much to discover in the nooks and crannies where most never thought to look.

"Bedridden?" she pressed, careful to infuse her question with an appropriate level of concern. "Whatever happened?"

A house devoid of guests, its gardens not filled with lanterns and wandering merrymakers, staff intently focused upon their master. Hazard or opportunity? Her mind whirled, calculating the distance from The Swan Inn to Batcote Hall. Two, perhaps three miles? Walkable. In a pair of sensible shoes. Which were in her travel trunk only a flight of stairs, a hallway and a closed door away.

"From the very beginning, it was a cursed house party," answered the Tudor courtier. "A near accident during the pheasant shoot, a burr lodged beneath a horse saddle, an angry black cat trapped in Lord Wraxall's dressing chamber." His gaze slid past Diana, a sheepish acknowledgement that her status as "unsuitable for marriage" had relegated her family to local accommodations, their invitation limited to the costumed ball. A common occurrence, though the sting had not lessened over time.

"How very gothic." Aurora leaned in, lightly touching the man's arm, encouraging him to continue.

Diana held her breath, hoping for more detail.

"Pages ripped from an overwrought novel," the courtier agreed, smiling. "But true disaster arrived in the form of farm equipment, involving an engine, a pipe release valve and scalding water. A late sowing of winter rye, though aether only knows why a baron felt the need to drive the steam tractor into the barn himself on the very evening he was to host a costume ball. Instead, the town physician attends his bedside."

"Is Lord Wraxall expected to recover?" Their mother sagged into a chair beside the fireplace, held upright only by the enormous volume of boiled starch that saturated the silk flowers and vines that twined about her green gown. Terra Mater, Mother Earth, had pinned too many hopes on the baron's personal, handwritten invitation.

"Too soon to know," the courtier replied. "But the evening's festivities are, necessarily, cancelled." He waved a hand toward the windowpanes. Beyond, a procession of polished carriages and gleaming clockwork horses rattled, clanked and clopped along High Street carrying house-guests away from Batcote Hall.

"What a shame." Aurora batted her eyelashes and tossed him a pearly smile, unable to suppress an instinct to flirt with a handsome gentleman despite the faceted yellow diamond engagement ring that adorned her finger. "And here I was looking forward to sinking my teeth into a candied apple."

The man all but swallowed his tongue.

"Behave," Diana whispered, with a pinch to the back of her sister's arm that elicited a yelp and a grateful glance from their mother. Aurora's wedding was but weeks away,

4

and the wealthy industrialist who'd slid that ring onto her finger bristled in the company of fawning gentlemen with the audacity to address his fiancée with any manner of familiarity. Theirs was a love match threaded with jealousy that only seemed to fuel the fire of their romance.

From their mother's point of view, the sooner the wedding, the better. Lest another sister fall into ruin before her future was secured.

Irritated, Diana pulled back her shoulders. Hers was a regrettable mistake, one that refused to stay in the past, following her from one society event to another, forever nipping at her heels, while the other half of the guilty parties suffered no such consequences. Her only consolation was the knowledge that Hector Godfrey and his wife did not number among the houseguests, though it rankled that her rival had been invited at all.

Impossible to forget the evil spark that had flared in his beady eyes when he'd overheard her conversation with Mr. Rachet in the museum's Shell Gallery—curse his booming voice—describe the contents of a letter sent to him some twenty years past. As such, the same bare bones facts had also been made available to Hector.

Earlier, a stroll through the village had brought the three of them within eyeshot, an exchange of narrow-eyed and cold glares their only interaction. But it was enough to know her nemesis possessed the same goal, that he would seek to thwart her every effort with the baron. As always, the prize was publication. This time, however, the stakes were higher, with no guarantee either of them would win.

A competition halted, or at least delayed, by the lord's misfortune.

Unless...

"Many guests adjourn to the ballroom of the Bristol Royal Hotel, though that is quite a distance away," the courtier continued. "A few plan to attend All Hallows' Eve festivities in the town's assembly hall, a location not more than a few steps along the High Street. Might I offer to escort three beautiful ladies to this local venue?" He crooked an arm.

Grinning, Aurora rose onto her toes, but Mother quickly dashed her hopes. "How very gallant of you, sir, but I'm afraid we must decline." She pressed a limp hand to her forehead. "I fear I'm developing a megrim and must retire for the evening. Nothing will bring me more comfort than the company of my daughters."

"Our loss. May your ills past swiftly." The courtier executed a bow worthy of Henry VIII at Hampton Court Palace then took his leave.

"Shall I order a bath sent up to your room?" Diana asked.

With a nod, Mother gathered up the layers of petals and tendrils that comprised her gown and stood, pointing her slippers in the direction of the staircase. Aurora sighed, her radiance dimming as she moved to follow, disappointed at her lost chance to play matchmaker for her sister.

Diana caught her elbow and spoke in a low voice. "I will be out this evening. Cover for me."

"It's only fair, I suppose." Aurora cast a longing glance toward High Street. "Perhaps there will be landed gentlemen in attendance."

A remark with which many would agree. At Diana's advanced age of twenty-five, the expectation was that matrimonial exertions ought to be her focus, not the composition of yet another paper detailing the ancient familial relationships of gastropods as defined by the conispiral torsion of the perpendicular axis of the foot.

"I'll not be at the assembly hall," she clarified, her pulse leaping, "but further afield. I've work to accomplish, not play. Tonight presents a shrinking window of opportunity." For tomorrow a train would carry them to Birmingham where the flurry of Aurora's wedding preparations would resume. If she didn't set out on this adventure, if she didn't at least attempt to locate the lost treasure, Diana would forever regret the lost opportunity.

"Wait." Her sister drew up straight and her eyebrows slammed together. "This is about the snail?"

"In part." Diana smiled, pressing a hand to her chest. Behind her bodice hung a pendant of amorphous amber. Embedded within the fossilized tree resin was a tiny, sinistral gastropod. They'd bickered, earlier, when Aurora wished to borrow it for the evening, arguing the necklace was the perfect ornament that would complete her sun costume.

Diana had categorically refused.

"What if you're caught?" Aurora wrapped a hand about her wrist, frowning. "It's theft, you realize, to remove property—yes, even seashells—from another's home."

She glared at her sister. They were more than seashells, and Aurora knew it.

Why else would Diana write letter after letter to the current Lord Wraxall, all but begging for permission to examine the neglected collection housed within his walls? Months of silence passed with a dozen or so missives ignored. She'd all but given up hope. Then a simple invitation to an All Hallows' Eve ball had arrived upon plain stationery—but with no additional note to suggest he might permit her access to his uncle's notebooks or shells. What was a scientific woman to make of such a response?

"It would be a rescue mission," she argued aloud. A thrill ran down her spine at the idea of carting away the entire collection in the dark of night. Yet, with any luck, there would be far too much for a single woman to carry. And her sister was correct. "But proper documentation matters. I've no intention of removing anything without Lord Wraxall's express permission." She twisted her lips. Well, perhaps a single sheet of paper. Possibly a notebook. Assuming, of course, she could locate the documentation she sought. "The current scenario makes my actions all the more pressing. If the baron dies without issue, who knows what might become of his uncle's collection while attempts are made to contact some distant relation?"

"Stop. I'm begging you." Aurora released her, then held up a hand. "Go. Only be certain not to be caught. If you cause a hullabaloo that ruins my wedding, my first act as a wealthy married woman will be to banish you to a cottage on the Dorset coast. There, you can hunt fossils to your heart's content."

"But the best snail fossils are in Barton on Sea in Hampshire!" she protested.

Her sister's eyebrows lifted, their peaks imbuing her face with a hint of evil. "Exactly."

A sharp reminder of how little value her mother and sister placed on Diana's academic pursuits. As if she needed more motivation to strike out on her own tonight.

～

LEO AWAKENED moments before the sun went down. Torture, that tiny window set high in the stone wall. A glimpse of the distant sun, one that lasted long enough to chart the orb's position and know that it was, yet again, October thirty-first. Then it slipped behind the garden wall, signaling the approach of twilight. His gaze inevitably fell next upon the face of a wall clock that read eight o'clock.

Every. Single. Time.

How many times must he relive this cursed evening? Once he'd loved this hidden laboratory, tucked away where few dared disturb him. But now? Now he couldn't even light a damned candle to relieve the dark until the last crepuscular rays flickered and died.

Died.

A most frustrating incident. One impossible to have anticipated.

Worse, he could recall foggy snippets of the night to come. He'd been coaxing the mucin to polymerize all evening and the glycosylated protein was on the precipice of forming a hydrogel when the fatal interruption had occurred.

All he wanted was to complete that work, yet time and again his every effort failed.

He glared at his semi-transparent fingers, passed them through the clear glass of an Erlenmeyer flask, sighed. A few more minutes, then he'd try again.

Clasping his hands behind his back, he rocked onto his heels and tipped his head back, counting the snails that crept across the floor, walls and ceiling while they left glis-

9

tening trails behind them to mark their passage. Thank aether the creatures loved the damp, dark and decaying. Not only were the gastropods a necessity, they were his only companions. He snorted. Tucked beneath the ground, this space was as silent as a grave. Which it almost was, save nowhere within the cool chamber had he found any bones. A relief, really, not to have his own skull staring back at him with empty sockets.

The darkness intensified.

Leo snapped his fingers and smiled as the sound echoed around him. It was time.

He pinched a match from his workbench and offered up a quiet plea that it was not too damp to ignite, then struck it. Relief rode his exhale, and he touched flame to wick.

A small circle of light radiated outward, illuminating an oddly dust-free workspace. That missing feature bothered him to no end. He cut another notch into the wood of the table. Twenty-three marks in total. By his count, it ought to be 1885. But without dust, without a dead body or bloodstains to confirm his own death, he couldn't shake the supposition that it might still be 1862.

CHAPTER TWO

THROUGHOUT THE VILLAGE, masked and costumed revelers roamed in bands of various sizes. Those in more extravagant ensembles converged upon the entryway of the assembly hall, calling greetings. Those of a more nightmarish variety—witches, ghosts, demons and individuals who wore alarming, featureless masks—carried hollowed-out turnip lanterns as they traipsed from house to house, singing for apples, ale or soul cakes in a lamenting tone that sent shivers running down her spine.

For a while, she walked among them, content to mingle, to blend, to move about unremarked as they neared the village outskirts. There, as she stepped away, a boy passed her an apple, wishing her good mischief. And with that, Diana found herself alone, hurrying along an increasingly deserted road, half-expecting a carriage ferrying Hector to the baron's home to overtake her at any moment.

With a startling abruptness, village became farmland. Scattered across the countryside, bonfires sparked to life, warding off evil spirits as the boundary between this world and another thinned, permitting souls of both the dead and living to stand upon the same threshold this cross-quarter night.

Wishing no attention from spirits or otherwise, Diana pulled the hood of her cape over her celestial crown and wrapped its folds about her shoulders, blotting out any stray beams of moonlight that might give sparkle to the constellations upon her gown. The night embraced her, and she quickened her steps, all but melting into the surrounding darkness as gusts of wind plucked at her clothing and whispered words of doubt into her ears.

Was this madness, setting out alone in the dark, tramping through the unfamiliar countryside with only the barest semblance of a plan? All to gaze upon the shells of creatures gathered from far corners of the globe? Her sister ought to have insisted she remain at the inn.

Too bold for her own good.

Pig-headed persistence.

Intractably academic and bookish.

Such were the phrases hurled at her after the incident, ones not entirely inaccurate. She'd dealt with heartache by finding a new interest. All her passion was now reserved for malacology, the study of mollusks, and it had served her well. How many women of her age had presented four well-received papers to the Zoological Society of London? She was so very close to winning membership and acceptance as an expert. But to do so, she needed to present truly groundbreaking work. Difficult when one was an unmarried woman not possessed of a small fortune permitting one to effortlessly travel the world.

She rejected the wind's whispered warnings of disaster and disappointment. Not madness, but determination. The path to glory was often strewn with obstacles and risk, and she was nearly there. No accolades were won by those who turned back when success was within reach. Passion and perseverance powered forward momentum.

One booted foot after the other, she tromped onward.

At last, Batcote Hall came into view. A great lawn stretched before her, sliced in half by a broad gravel-covered drive. A single steam-powered carriage rested before the hall, attended to by a bored, disinterested groom. An attending physician?

Best to avoid wide open spaces where both moonlight and lamplight might cast her into a curious shadow, a decision at odds with her strained assertion that, if caught, the invitation in her reticule might somehow excuse her behavior. But she had everything to gain and nothing to lose. She moved along the lawn's woodland edge until ivy-covered stone rose beside her. If zoological society rumor was to be believed, the treasure she sought was in the building's library, a room to the left of the front entrance. She faced its side window now.

Could she climb the few feet? No way to know but to try. Hood pulled low, Diana dashed across the lawn.

Skirts hiked and secured, she tugged at the vines, testing the strength of the woody stems. How very delightful that no one had worried that the growth of a century and a half might propel sneak thieves into their midst. With a smirk, she reached overhead to wrap her fingers about the highest, thickest vines.

And quickly found she'd overestimated her abilities. An expert she might be at scrabbling up and down rocky English coastlines, but this ivy resented her intrusion. Various tendrils and woody bits caught at the folds of her skirt, at her spangles. Worse, the shoots and stems shifted and bowed with her every movement.

Twice, she nearly plummeted back to the ground. Snarling, Diana hauled herself upward, at last reaching the window. She peered inside. A single gas jet burned, tossing more shadows than light. But she'd located the library. From floor to ceiling were walls covered with books, so many that a narrow balcony encircled the room.

A wave of envy swept over her. Imagine having such a treasure to oneself. And well she might, she mentally slapped herself, if Lord Wraxall agreed to sponsor her project. At least for a short time. But first, she needed to avoid being caught.

She pushed at the window sash. Small favors, it was unlocked.

A final skirmish with the ancient ivy ensued before Diana managed to somersault into the room, landing in a disgraceful heap upon a thick, hand knotted Turkish rug. Muffled though her tumble had been, her heart pounded, insisting that at any moment a steambot might sound the alarm. She pushed to her feet and stood, listening intently for the rattle and clack of mechanical wheels.

When none came, she tossed back her hood, then shook

out her skirts, frowning at the damage done to her constellations. One of the Seven Sisters was missing and there was a tear in Orion's belt. She hoped the fabric and celestial sacrifice was worth it.

Time to snoop.

From her reticule, she drew a small bioluminescent sphere. Vigorous shaking rudely awakened the dormant bacteria within—she imagined the tiny creatures throwing out rays of blue-white light in a glare of displeasure. Her star-studded crown showcased a crescent moon at its center, one resting upon its side. Behind it, twists of wire formed a hollow into which she inserted the miniature globe, adjusting the phase of the crown's moon to full. Perfect for the goddess Diana.

A beacon, of sorts. Ostensibly to draw the notice of eligible young men in a crowded ballroom, it also served as a hands-free light source.

She swept bioluminescent moonbeams over the empty library. Where to begin? Not with the leather-bound tomes that lined the walls. Tempting though they might be, such books contained only published information. What she needed was raw data with which to make a splash and not so much as a case or a box was tucked among their spines.

A search of the ground level revealed nothing promising except a tall cabinet of drawers set against the far wall. Breathless, she darted across the room to tug at its handles only to have her expectations crushed. Though the drawers slid forth to reveal a collection, there was not a trace of calcium carbonate aside from the occasional mother-of-pearl inlay. Instead of shells or fossils, she found an array of telescopes, astrolabes, sextants and a number of other astronomical devices to which she could not begin to put a name lay within, all carefully nested in velvet. Most of them gleamed brightly, save a few sporting rusty edges from time spent in use outdoors—the weathered style of a brass sundial, for example.

Frustrated, she spun about. Hopes of discovering a forgotten malacological horde were fast fading. Perhaps above, upon the balcony resting in a shadowy corner? It *had* been twenty-three years since Lord Leopold Wraxall returned from his worldwide wanderings. Perhaps his heir, focused as he was upon more recent scientific advancements, had no time for such dusty relics?

Hand upon the iron railing of a spiral staircase, she climbed upward. But found only disappointment. More books and yet more books. Not a box or case among them. Dammit. Was that why the current lord so long ignored her letters? He regarded her missives as pleadings of an insane woman demanding access to data that didn't exist?

No. She refused to believe it. Why else invite two rival zoologists to the same gathering?

She huffed, sending a plume of dust billowing into the air and startling an overlarge beetle. It scurried with haste to dive under a bookcase.

Under?

Why was there a gap, some ten feet in the air, beneath a bookcase? Bent at the hips, she cast her light along a long door-width crack. Could it be? A hidden door to a hidden room? Excitement fizzled and bubbled through her veins. Straightening, she pushed at the bookcase. Nothing. Might it be a matter of pulling the right book?

She reached for *Essays on the Microscope,* by George Adams, the left uppermost book and tugged. The tome fell into her hand, but nothing shifted.

The library door opened, flooding the lower level with light. "The archived records validated hearsay, but no specifics were documented. Our client requires specific, in-depth details. Any pertinent notes are likely to be found here, hidden in the library. Search the shelves, not a single book remains unexamined. Bring me anything handwritten."

That voice! It pierced her skin, immobilizing her like venom from a cone snail. Hector Godfrey. Once she'd hung on his every word. No more.

Diana wanted to scream.

Instead, she jerked into motion, yanking her hood into place, extinguishing the glow of her moon and crouching to wrap her cloak about her dress. Making herself smaller in his presence, something she'd sworn to never do again. But here, far from the erudite gatherings of the London Zoological Society, there was nothing to gain and everything to lose by revealing her presence.

How unfair that he, along with an assistant, managed to enter Batcote Hall by means of a door. Bribery of an enterprising servant, no doubt, who saw a way to profit while his employer lay on this deathbed.

Wait.

Hector only hunted for handwritten notes? She frowned. What of the fossils, the shells? Without them, it would be impossible to publish. Another term bothered her: client. Precious few individuals would be inclined to pay so much as a shilling for undocumented data.

"Every book?" another man said. "That's a mad proposition. It'll take hours."

"We've all night." A beam of light swept the room. "If the notes aren't here, we move on to the attics, storerooms. Rummage about until there's not a nook or cranny left unexplored. If Miss Starr dares to show her face—"

"Yes, boss. As discussed. Bound and gagged and stowed in the carriage, though I still think—"

"No more thinking," Hector snapped. "You've done nothing but bungle every attempt. I hired you to arrange an accident that would incapacitate, not kill. You went too far, sabotaging the steam tractor. If the baron dies, if murder charges are brought up—" His words cut off. "What's this?"

Accident? Sabotage? Her stomach roiled. What information contained within those notes could be of such value that Hector considered criminal acts justifiable?

Diana peered over the railing. Bathed in moonlight beside the open library window, Hector held a swatch of spangled satin, cloth ripped from the hem of her gown. She cringed at the thought of such incriminating evidence falling into his hands. How many had seen her with her sister tonight? Would anyone recall? Nonetheless, steps would need to be taken to dispose of her costume. Assuming she managed to escape undetected.

"Someone's been here," he concluded. "Diana?"

A suffocating tidal wave of dread washed over her, and she fell backward against the shelves. Hector would seek revenge for every word she'd ever uttered against him, and there was no hope of eluding him. He would find her and soon. Then, without witnesses, his options were limitless.

She forced herself onto hands and knees. If she could reach the stairs, descend quickly, there was a slight chance she might reach the door before he laid hands upon her. She would scream if necessary.

Her elbow jammed into the spine of a large book. Beside her, the bookcase moved. *Illustrations of The Fossil Conchology of Great Britain and Ireland* by Thomas Brown. Could escape be at hand? Her heart pounded. She pushed at the red spine of the book, bracing for a loud screech. None came. Inch by inch the bookshelf shifted, pivoting open. *Thank aether.* Holding her breath, she crawled through the secret doorway, then pushed with trembling hands.

Snick. The latch caught.

Only then did she toss back her hood and turn to see what hand luck had dealt.

Ding!

Leo's head snapped up, his gaze drawn to a brass bell hanging from a vibrating coil of metal. An alert system he'd installed ages ago to warn him if—or when—someone discovered the secret passageway.

He blinked, then let out a bark of laughter. This was the first variation in his All Hallows' Eve routine in—according to the notches in his workbench—twenty-three years. Experiment forgotten, he straightened, ran his hands through his hair and began to pace. An alteration in the pattern, what could it mean? Might he not be doomed to repeat the same evening over and over for time immemorial?

Were there other deviations from the norm?

Closing his eyes, Leo picked at his memory, cataloging every variable, weighing every detail in the balance. His location, standing in the middle of his laboratory. The sun's position in the sky. The hands of the clock. The locations of the various snails as plucked from the damp stone to drop into the glass terrarium.

Nothing, no deviations from any other night.

Eyes open, he scanned the chamber. Not a stick of furniture out of place. Candles burning where he'd lit them that very first evening. The enormous gears that opened and closed the entry into his workshop motionless and still beside shelving that held bits and pieces of various astronomical contraptions his grandfather had set aside to repair. He crossed to the corner of the room and bent to look through the eyepiece of his grandfather's telescope, but the view of the night sky it provided was the same as always.

Unpacked crates from his worldwide travels were still stacked in the corner, undisturbed. Upon arriving, he'd only pried the lid off one crate, the one holding the *Asperitas striata* snails. Live specimens, no matter how carefully their requirements had been met, suffered mightily when subjected to long voyages. Set free, the faintly glowing snails had taken to his sunken laboratory with alacrity, traipsing about with abandon. A few, he recalled, had even managed to slip through gaps in the masonry, intent upon an open-air excursion in the garden.

Garden.

Heat crept up his back and settled beneath his collar.

Focused upon completing his experiment as key to escaping this non-existence, he'd not once thought to look out the window to see how—if—the Southeast Asian snails had taken to the English climate.

Not once had he thought to vary his tactics. And him, a decorated soldier. How embarrassing.

He searched his mind for other forgotten factors that might alter the fabric of his past and current reality.

There was the letter he'd sent Mr. Rachet, a rising malacologist, inviting him to visit Batcote Hall, to view the vast collection of mollusk fossils and shells—all carefully documented as to their date, location, and habitat—that he had hauled home.

Leo had planned to set up a display in the library of select specimens, one that would awe the man. All intended to entice Mr. Rachet to aid him with what would be a massive project of classification and identification, generating many monographs. The grand incentive? A jointly published volume, perhaps two, complete with colored illustrations.

But Leo had died before a response arrived.

Hadn't he?

He twisted his lips, at a loss as to who might have discovered the hidden door in the library after twenty-three years. Unless... it was still 1862 and tonight was yet another iteration? His nephew Leon was clever and curious and showed much promise—Leo had been meaning to take the child under his wing—and might have found the passageway on his own. Perhaps it was him? Past, present, future—impossible to know where he fell on the timeline.

Pinching the bridge of his nose, Leo blew out a breath. *Window.* He ought to look out the window. It mocked him, the stool, as he lifted it, set it below the dark glass panes, and climbed atop to peer out into the walled garden searching for snails.

There, he spotted one. And another, and another. So many, the quantity of snails was impossible to tally. The chances the bioluminescent gastropods had managed to reproduce so successfully in the short time since he'd last observed them in the garden were so minuscule as to be laughable. Moreover, the slow-growing yew tree was thicker at the base, its branches spread more widely over the headstones of his ancestors. More had joined their number, among which he suspected his was counted.

Twenty-three years had indeed passed, at least outside of this room.

Time during which he had not courted a woman, had sired no children, had not returned to London or contributed to the founding of a new medical school, one prioritizing research.

His shoulders sagged as a hollow feeling carved at his innards. He was nothing but an empty shell, locked in a forgotten chamber. Powerless, save to repeat the past. How very discouraging. Ought he just settle onto his pallet, light his hookah and enjoy the evening allowing his residual energy to gradually diminish in amplitude? What point in pursuing his research, if the end result could never be reached, the final product never distributed to those in need?

Ring! Another warning bell sounded.

Leo's eyebrows slammed together as he refocused, staring across the garden to the grotto, eager to be proven wrong. Breathless—a ridiculous state of being for a ghost—he waited, wondering who might emerge from the passageway to take a nighttime stroll among his snails.

CHAPTER THREE

*A*SECRET PASSAGEWAY.
  Tucked into the walls of Batcote Hall.
But leading where?

Excitement swirled together with apprehension, and her heart tapped a swift beat against her sternum sending blood rushing through her veins. As returning to the library was not an option, Diana put one foot in front of the other, brushing away curtains of cobwebs cast in a milky blue light by the artificial moonbeams of her celestial crown.

Ignoring a right turn that likely led to the private quarters of a resident, she pointed her toes straight ahead. The walls closed in. A flight of stairs led downward. A right-angled turn, then a steep drop, after which wooden overhead beams were replaced by an arch of stone. Another long, narrow corridor. A left turn and—

Diana drew to a halt. Before her, a deep dark shaft dropped into darkness. Embedded in the wall, an iron ladder. She swallowed hard, then pressed a hand to the rough wall, leaning forward, dipping her chin that her light source might reveal its depth. Below she spied a landing, the surface of which resembled packed dirt.

An underground tunnel that would aid in her escape? Disappointment pulled at her shoulders. Not to a secret chamber, then, where the former lord had stashed his hidden hoard. She heaved a great sigh and reached for the topmost rung. Was that a gust of fresh air? If this secret passageway offered escape, she would trust herself to its many zigs and zags. Anything was better than being caught by Hector or his henchman.

She arrived at the bottom, cast the roots overhead a brief grimace, the support beams a glare of mistrust, then ducked, hurrying along the tunnel. Cool air swirled about her and the ground sloped upward, promising the end was near.

At last, rough-hewn stone stairs led upward to a door. She pushed at the old wood and emerged from the underground tunnel to find herself in a recessed grotto set into the stone of a walled garden. In its center, a small family chapel squatted beside what must be the family's burial ground, a cluster of headstones gathered under an ancient yew tree. Lost in wonder beneath a canopy of bare autumn branches with the night sky glittering down upon her, the click of the door latching behind her barely registered.

Before conscious thought reached her higher brain centers, Diana had set off upon a gravel path that circled about the yew tree, leading her before the two newest graves.

Lord Marcus Wraxall (1834–1883), the current lord's

recently deceased father and younger brother of Lord Leopold Wraxall, Veteran of the Crimean War and Explorer (1832–1862). She reached upward, snapping off a sprig of yew to set upon the gravestone, paying her respect to the man she'd hoped might prove to be her personal academic savior.

She frowned, wondering what was recorded in the man's notes that Hector was so desperate to discover. Nothing she'd learned about Leopold Wraxall suggested his collection was stored elsewhere, but given she'd failed to find so much as a box containing a single shell within his library, it was not a possibility she could dismiss. Not all malacological rumor reached her ears. Regardless, if Hector was caught rummaging through Wraxall possessions without permission, his actions would be judged poorly in light of the lord's condition and brought to the attention of the authorities.

That scenario tipped the corners of her tight lips upward into the semblance of a smile.

If only.

The treasure existed, of that she was certain. If tucked in some long-forgotten corner. And the only specimen ever to see the light of day hung about her neck. The jeweler who sold her the gemstone claimed to have purchased it from Lord Wraxall himself, a reluctant sale made to finance the final leg of his trip home.

Preserved in amber, the tiny snail embedded within appeared to be an ancestor of the cyclophoridae, a family of terrestrial snails. If so, hers might be the oldest of its species ever found. Yet without written documentation, Diana could prove nothing.

A burst of laughter rode in on a gust of cold air, and she spun, searching for its source. There, beyond the bars of an iron gate, a distant bonfire burned. Men, women and children gathered nearby, celebrating the fall festival.

Heaving a sigh, Diana plucked the moon from her crown and snuffed its light in the black void of her reticule. Beneath the shadow of the great yew, she waited for her eyes to adjust to the dark. No point in drawing attention to her unauthorized wanderings. She hated to abandon her plans, but what choice remained but to return to The Swan Inn? To tangle, yet again, with Hector would, at best, serve only to tarnish her sister's wedding plans and, at worse, find the next victim of an "unfortunate" accident.

Flash.

Diana blinked, rubbed her eyes.

Flash.

What was the source, glow worms? No, it was far too late in the season. Moreover, these creatures did not emit a steady light, they blinked.

She scanned the gardens. Another flash. And another and another. Bioluminescent light flickered and pulsed all about her. Fixing her gaze upon the location of a single flash, she summoned patience, tracking it—step by step—to its source: a small, brown-shelled snail.

Gently, she lifted the tiny creature onto her palm. Jaw agape, she studied the unusual gastropod. To her knowledge, which was extensive, no land snail was known to produce a biological light. Small, no more than an inch and a half in length, the brown shell possessed an uncommon sinistral curl, a twist of whorls that rose to the left.

The yellow-green light emitted was confined to the location of the snail's head, emanating from a region just behind its mouth. Genus *Asperitas*, perhaps, species unknown. But such was only a guess without first tabulating its features and comparing them to those listed in a taxonomy text.

Had Lord Wraxall carried this unknown species home with him? If so, how had it lived—no, flourished—inside a walled garden for some twenty-three years without anyone taking notice?

Whilst contemplating these deep questions, Diana walked along the gravel pathway as it circled counterclockwise, about the small chapel and the graveyard, moving in and out of the yew's shadow. All about her—in the tall grass, upon the stone walls, snails climbed, flashing out an indecipherable message.

Her steps led her to an iron gate with rust-pitted bars—where she found herself loathe to leave the garden's embrace.

These snails that traipsed about within its walls could be the scientific discovery that would set the top-hat-wearing zoologists back on their heels, forcing them to recognize her as an expert, to count her among their number. Save her discovery was likely secondhand, one made by a man who had died under mysterious circumstances some two decades past. And publication without being able to cite sources or name the snails' geographical origin was worse than pointless.

Nothing to do, save pray Hector only searched the Batcote Hall, not the grounds themselves, that Lord Wraxall recovered and—miracle of miracles—responded to her as-yet unwritten letter in writing, granting her access to his uncle's collection and the snails within his walled garden. Only then might she return and conduct a proper survey.

With a sigh approaching a growl, she pulled at the iron gate's latch.

It didn't budge.

She yanked hard enough to set the hinges rattling and clanking, but the gate was locked tight.

A frustrated scream rose to clog her throat, but she swallowed it. Would nothing go her way tonight?

Again, she circled the garden, searching its walls for another means of egress, but there were no vines or trellis-work providing likely options. No matter how hard she pushed at the wooden door inside the hidden grotto, it too refused to open. She scowled at the green man carved into the arch who blocked her return to the hall, but it was probably for the best that she not retrace those steps.

At last, she stopped before Lord Wraxall's gravestone. "What to do?" she asked the man in a huff. "A discovery such as yours ought to be announced to the world, but without documentation, without the permission of the estate, my hands are tied." She set the snail down upon his grave. "You're correct, sir. Call for help and pray no one mistakes my howls for that of a demon."

One last time, she circled the garden, a final tour to appreciate the malacological wonder that thrived within its walls. All about her, the air seemed to shimmer, the moon beamed down upon her as stars twinkled, all while the blinking snails continued their clockwise pilgrimage, a decided oddity.

When she reached the gate, she tried the latch once

more. Still stuck as firmly as before. Diana drew a deep breath, prepared to scream until help arrived. With luck, the gardener would release her, but ask no questions in his haste to hurry back to ale, apples and fireside ghost stories.

Wait.

Where were the bonfires? Minutes ago, they'd burned brightly. Now, they were extinguished. Not a soul raised a voice in celebration or otherwise.

Her jaw snapped shut. Had Lord Wraxall died? *Aether.* She spun about, back pressed to the inner wall, contemplating the impropriety of drawing attention to herself at such a juncture. Yet it had to be done, lest her sister send a search party for her come dawn.

Amidst this mental turmoil, awareness of changes within the garden came upon her gradually. No snails blinked. The yew tree's branches no longer extended quite so far over the burial ground. And a window set into the chapel's foundation emitted faint, flickering light—and from behinds its glass panes, a face stared back.

A shiver ran down her spine.

Thunder boomed, and she raised her face toward the night sky. Angry, dark clouds gathered overhead where minutes before stars had twinkled in a cloudless sky.

There was no such thing as magic, no such thing as the thinning of the veil on All Hallows' Eve.

No such things as ghosts.

And yet...

TREMBLING, the star-clad woman took a step in his direction. Then another, and another.

While he'd watched, the garden's glow snails, ones he'd christened *Asperitas striata*, winked out of existence. Two gravestones faded from view. And thunder boomed as clouds scudded across the moon, signaling the arrival of a storm that he'd not heard save the very night he—

Could the legend be true?

Thrice 'round the old yew tree to tear the veil of time and fate.

Certainly, he and Marcus had attempted the ritual on All Hallows' Eve as boys, careful to pack provisions, to leave their parents with a carefully crafted note should their beds be found empty on the morrow, and to follow every last instruction whispered by the old hermit who lived in the woods.

Not a thing had happened, save an overindulgence in glazed apples and roasted nuts and the acquisition of a head cold that had lasted near to a week.

But this woman, ambling about, managed to circle the ancient graveyard yew almost by accident, changing—what exactly?

Was he free? Leo ran across the room, reaching for the lever that would activate the staircase mechanism, but his hand passed straight through it.

Dammit.

Still cursed, still trapped. The circumnavigation of the garden had altered reality, both hers and his, but how exactly remained unclear. He paced the chamber, mentally cataloguing everything again, and finding not a thing out of place.

Outside, a flash of lightning was followed by a crack of thunder, then the skies unleashed a torrential downpour.

The woman's distressed cry met his ears, along with the sounds of rushed footsteps upon gravel.

A signal bell rang in his laboratory, then the chapel door closed with a *thunk*.

Leo ran his hands through his hair, locking fingers at the back of his neck as he stared at the speaking tube. Dare he use it?

If this woman came from the future, his voice would scare her witless.

Was it possible, time travel? Excluding that one night he and Marcus had set logic aside in an attempt to spin the clock's hands backward, Leo would have scoffed—with vehemence—at the suggestion of such a phenomena that was beyond the scope of scientific investigation.

Had he not watched her circumnavigate the chapel's yard, witnessed its transformation, he might still cling to disbelief. This, despite his existence outside of time, yet within it. A spirit formed of obstinate and enduring energy sustained by unfinished business.

He glanced at his workbench, at the problem he was attempting to solve.

Witness to an unending procession of death and disease in the Crimean War, he'd undertaken an expedition to Southeast Asia in an effort to expunge the horror from his mind, to find new purpose. Fossil and shell hunting had proved a suitable distraction—until the horrific accident aboard the steamer ship at sea. A boiler explosion had killed ten instantly and scalded seventeen. Never had he seen such severe burns: red and peeling, swollen and blistered, clothing charred and fused to skin. He'd done all he could to ease the pain and suffering, to help them heal. But only two men had survived.

After that, Leo had almost abandoned his journey. But for a chance encounter with a local healer, for the reintroduction to an old treatment presented in a new light, at that juncture he would have returned to his Somerset estate to molder in the countryside, a useless, aging baron content to let his brother's son continue on as his presumed heir. Instead, he'd returned with new purpose, ruffling Edith's feathers and paying the ultimate price for his years-long dereliction of family duties.

On every last All Hallows' Eve, his inevitable demise arrived a few hours hence. A time point still in the future. With the pattern broken, might it not arrive at all? Unwise to assume so, though he would certainly make the attempt. However, this woman, if convinced to aid his efforts, might present an opportunity to send his work into the future, regardless of the evening's ultimate outcome.

For several long minutes, he waited. For her heart to stop racing, for her skirts to cease dripping onto the floorboards, for her to take in the vaulted ceiling and the curious astronomical contraption of rings and stars and planets that hung overhead. Did she also stare at the bowl of milk and a dish of nuts, at the apples and soul cakes laid atop the altar? A decidedly pagan practice to appease either fairies, the dead or both. No one had ever seemed quite certain.

He cleared his throat, unpracticed as it was, then pulled

the cork stopper from the speaking tube. "Good evening, Miss—?"

Dead silence met his ears.

How to convince this woman that he was not a malevolent spirit? Well, a spirit, perhaps. One who could be spiteful at times, but none of his ire would be aimed in her direction.

"Please, I assure you I'm alive, merely trapped in my workshop. A stuck gear, you see... If you could assist?" All little white lies. Or were they? "There's a copper pipe behind the altar in the corner of the chapel from which my voice emanates. If you speak into it, I'll be able to hear your reply."

A long hesitation, then a cautious voice echoed down. "To whom am I speaking?"

Ah, a tricky question. She'd set a small object upon his gravestone, an object now missing from the churchyard. "Leo will do. In front of you, there's a lever that opens a door. It's buried within the dials and knobs and levers. If you could reach behind the red knob marked 'Mars' and pull the third from the left?"

"Lord Leopold Wraxall, born in 1832?"

So there would be no escaping the truth. "Indeed."

Another pause. "And the year is?"

He sighed. "1862."

"Returned from your voyages. Might your workshop hold a number of crates, the contents of which are of a zoological nature?"

She knew of him. Of his trip. Had his reputation traveled beyond his grave? It must have. Pride swelled, but was quickly squashed as he recalled the high likelihood of his imminent demise. "It does. If you're inclined to examine the items, pull that lever, and I'll pry the lid off the crate of your choice."

"You're alone?"

"Highly improper, I'm aware, but I see no way to rectify this situation. Chaperones are in short supply this All Hallows' Eve, but I promise to conduct myself as a gentleman."

"And as a scientist?"

Leo glanced at his crates. They'd sat in the far corner, abandoned. What might lure such a young woman, a presumed zoologist, to hunt for them in his workshop after all these years? "Of course. If you'll pull the lever..."

Curiosity overcame her caution. *Clank, click, clink.* As the counterweight dropped, the teeth of numerous gears fell into place and began to turn. Lengths of chain rattled, dropping flagstones into the floor at various depths, each supported by iron bars that slid outward from slots in the workshop's wall, forming a narrow staircase.

He attempted to climb upward, that he might greet the lady properly, but found he could not—no matter how much effort he expended—lift a single foot onto the lowermost stair. He was still trapped in time, his fate yet unaltered.

Leo held his breath, waiting. Worried good sense would prevail, that she would turn back.

Then a pagan moon goddess descended, stood before him, hair swept up in a loose chignon beneath a celestial crown, garbed in a midnight star-spangled gown that his many candles toiled to illuminate. Wet tendrils of hair were plastered to her cheeks and water dripped from her hem.

Soaked to the skin, but never before had he laid eyes upon such a vision.

Her eyes were inquisitive and questioning, set in a face of gentle curves that nonetheless managed to convey stubborn determination. Eyes that first glanced at the spoils of his voyage, at the snail-filled aquarium, before settling upon him. Most definitely a zoologist.

He swept a bow, as one does for... "The goddess Diana, I presume?"

CHAPTER FOUR

SHE'D BURST INTO THE old chapel seeking shelter from the rainstorm and found a curious blend of past and present. Simple offerings laid out atop an altar brought an ancient Celtic tradition inside a sanctuary. But the jaw-dropping feature was the enormous astronomical contraption that hung overhead, drawing the mind into a deep contemplation of the night sky.

A multitude of pipes and tubes branched and coiled over the walls, arching to converge upon a spherical framework of crisscrossing metal rings centered about the Earth, a Ptolemaic armillary sphere, that the principle circles of the heavens might be charted by equinoctial and ecliptic degrees. Yet within the brass frame of the skeletonized celestial globe was suspended an orrery. With the sun poised at the center, the planets were set to rotate upon the sphere of the elliptic.

An ambiguous arrangement, attempting to fit the Copernican planetary system within an Earth-centered armillary, but nonetheless a magnificent contraption. In and about the various rings, gears upon gears meshed that, when activated, the planets might chart their orbit about the sun beneath rotating heavenly spheres.

A striking attempt to blend the artistry of metal craft with science.

It hung motionless, but no less impressive.

Then a voice had echoed through the sanctuary, tipping her world further off balance.

"Lady Diana," she replied, automatically. "This can't be real. *You* can't be real. I must be dreaming." Her words echoed off the walls, contradicting her statement with fine auditory detail suggesting authenticity as did the roughness of the stone beneath her palm.

Now she was confronted with a ghost—one who bowed, no less, to welcome her by name—and stood before her in a chamber beneath a chapel beside a graveyard. One in which his coffin had rested a few minutes past. Before the world had shifted, spinning the hands of the clock backward some twenty-three years?

Impossible.

It had to be a dream.

Could one be cold, wet and shivering in a dream?

Perhaps she'd tripped and hit her head. Perhaps she lay beneath the old yew tree in a feverish state, hallucinating?

Wrapping her arms across her chest, Diana shook her head. "You can't possibly be real."

The cut of the waistcoat, the knot of the cravat, the fall of his trousers—all decades short of fashionable. Yet he was anything but an old man dressed in the clothing of his youth. The conjured Lord Leopold Wraxall cut quite the figure, one who had conveniently tossed his coat over the back of a divan. He was tall, with broad shoulders that stretched the fabric of his shirtsleeves and strained the buttons of his waistcoat.

She blushed as her gaze slipped lower. Her imagination had produced much to admire. Instead of striking terror into her heart, this revenant awakened desires she'd long ago thrown a blanket over and left for dead. Warmth stirred low in her stomach.

Diana snapped her head upward. Sapphire eyes the color of a deep, blue sea stared back. His tousled hair spiked outward in all directions—charming, if in a distracted manner, as if she'd interrupted him in the middle of some important project. An impression reinforced by the day's growth of stubble across a square jaw. A hint of mockery touched his full lips while the fine lines on his forehead above arched eyebrows suggested Leo suppressed amusement at her candid survey of his corporeal state.

Yes, Leo. Why bother with formal introductions under such circumstances?

Aether, she was trapped in a gothic novel, lusting after a ghost.

"On this uncanny night, I too am forced to suspend disbelief at your sudden appearance in my garden, in my workshop," Leo replied. "How fortunate I find myself, to discover that the scholarly help sent to me this All Hallows' Eve is as heavenly as the moon the stars above. Do your academic talents fall in paleontological pursuits or with the extant mollusks?"

A man who lauded her beauty, but was more interested

in her intellectual pursuits? This was a first. Her face grew warm. Surely his choice of words alone proved this was no more than mere fantasy?

"A little of both, but," she plucked at her sopping skirt and shot him a flirtatious glance, "I don't suppose you could produce dry clothing, or light a fire before we turn our attention to malacological matters?" Her subconscious had bestowed quite the gift. Might as well enjoy it.

"A fire?" He glanced over his shoulder at the small, iron wood stove tucked in a corner, bemused, as if he'd not noticed the pervasive chill. His space was well-suited to root vegetable storage, not so much human occupancy. "Your wish is my command, Lady Diana." He opened the door, struck a match and tossed it onto kindling already in place. From a steamer trunk, he produced a colorful, paisley smoking jacket, which he draped over his arm, eyebrows lifted in challenge. "Alas, I possess no convenient modesty screen."

Dream, she reminded herself, before unhooking the bodice of her gown. Before a man, if only an imaginary one. Brazen of her. "You'll not turn around?"

He tipped his head. "Did you want me to?"

"No, not particularly."

The answer shocked her. The handful of times she'd been unclothed before—beside? beneath?—a man, circumstances had been entirely different. At the house party, she'd engaged in much sneaking about, to her deep and everlasting regret. Many promises had been made, all of them broken. But not before she'd let that traitor into her bed and between her legs several nights in a row, an experience she would have deemed "adequate" if not for the knife he'd later stabbed into her back.

Diana peeled the wet fabric from her arms, tossed the bodice aside, then unhooked her skirts, shoving the sodden mess to the ground—and met Leo's appreciative gaze. Only then did bravery desert her.

Her eyes dropped to his large hands, rough and scarred and overwhelmingly attractive. Added to the obvious strength of broad wrists and corded forearms—both revealed by rolled back cuffs—and it was enough to make any woman burn for his touch.

When had her fantasies become so very detailed?

"You'll excuse me, my lady, for staring." Leo held open the smoking jacket. Diana slid into its welcome embrace, shivering as the pads of his fingers brushed over the bare skin of her shoulders, while the warmth of his breath drifted over the nape of her neck. Every nerve tingled with awareness.

If she leaned backward, ever so slightly, would he slide those hands of his down her arms, kiss the edge of her jaw and turn her into a full embrace?

Real. He felt altogether too real.

Was it possible this was no dream? "You're quite forgiven." Space. She needed space. She stepped away, if only a short distance, before turning.

His gaze dropped to her bosom. Then he laughed, running a hand over the stubble on his jaw. "I'd not thought to see that necklace again."

"This?" Her hand flew to her chest, where the amber pendant hung low upon its silver chain just above the edge of her corset, exposed by the removal of her wet gown. A touch of dismay wedged itself into her fantasy. So much for her imagination arranging an indiscretion. "A stunning piece, true, but what caught my eye was the tiny snail trapped within the resin and preserved for millions of years."

"Ah, yes." He brightened, though his gaze lingered ever so slightly before it lifted. "A woman after my own heart. Fitting that you were lured into my presence by the promise of malacological treasures crated and hauled back to British shores."

"Where, exactly, did you find such amber?" Diana stiffened her spine, reconciling herself to a meeting of minds and nothing else. Such was her lot. "Based on the inclusions, the Baltic region seems unlikely."

"Burma," he answered, glancing toward his workbench. "There was word of amber containing inclusions in the Hukawng Valley, so I detoured into mountains. I've more pieces," he waved at the crates, "among the fossils and shells. Most contain embedded arthropods, a few arachnids. Enough to support years of work and an untold number of zoological papers."

"Truly?" Now she lusted after nothing so much as a crowbar.

"Not to mention my discovery of a certain small brown snail, unremarkable by day."

She grinned. "But a bioluminescent wonder by night." The creatures had been in the garden—she'd witnessed the phenomena with her own two eyes—until they suddenly weren't. "Did so very few people know of your workshop that it would go undiscovered for—"

"Twenty-three years?" he asked, finishing her sentence.

"It was my grandfather's space first. He was an astronomer. When he wasn't working in the chapel above to recreate the known universe, he collected and restored all kinds of paraphernalia used to gaze at the stars and planets. After my death, it appears to have been forgotten."

That explained the shelving at the base of the stairs. Its boards bowed and bent beneath an odd assortment of dilapidated equipment. Easy enough to accept the presence of a workshop, if not the man before her.

"How?" She gaped. "How can you possibly be real?"

"An excellent question." He strode to his workbench, tapped its wooden surface. "At dusk on All Hallows' Eve, I awake, once again standing in the exact position I did on that same night in 1862. I can move about, but full dark must fall before I'm able to manipulate my environment, to light so much as a candle before I resume my work. I never do so without first carving a mark, save for that first evening." He caught her gaze.

"It is, after all, October 31st, 1885," she whispered, as if the date corresponding with a ghost's marks served to demystify the situation in the slightest. Aether, how she twisted logic to extract an explanation.

"Is it?" he countered. "Before your appearance in the garden, there were twenty-two grooves." He drew his fingertips across the smooth edge of the workbench. "Now, there are none. When you circled the yew three times, counterclockwise, you turned back time."

"Impossible." But a certain queasiness gripped Diana's stomach. She sank onto the settee. An abundance of legends centered about ancient churchyard yew trees. One particularly gruesome belief held that the roots of the yew twisted and twined though the empty eye sockets of the dead, keeping them secure in their graves. She shuddered. Certainly not a myth applicable to this situation.

"Once I would have agreed. Now?" He shook his head. "Twenty-three years ago, I died. Here," he slapped a palm down upon the workbench, "in this room. Twenty-three times I've relived that night. Tonight began the same as any other, until," he pointed at a brass bell that hung from a coiled spring, "you found the hidden door in my library."

"In your nephew's library," she countered. "In 1885."

"If I'm dead, if I die again tonight, then yes, my nephew's." Hands thrown wide, Leo paced from one end of the room to his desk and back. "But if it's 1862, who the rightful owner of Batcote Hall might be is still very much up for debate."

"Is it possible to stop your death, to alter the future?" Diana asked, unable to believe she was having such a conversation. The convolutions of logic were bewildering. "How do you—did you—die?" A complicated array of glassware shared space upon the workbench amidst glass bottles that held an untold number of chemical reagents. "A laboratory accident?"

"Not that," he snorted. "I was murdered. Stabbed in the back by the one person who knew I'd moved my work here to my grandfather's old workshop. I'm not surprised she denied the existence of my collection and turned away any who sought it out."

In the back? How treacherous!

"She?"

"Lady Edith Wraxall."

LADY DIANA FROZE. "The mother of the current lord?"

"The very same," he growled, irritated to learn she would not be held accountable for his murder. Justice had not been served. "Her family's property adjoins mine. When we were but children, our families came to an arrangement, agreeing that she and I should wed. Edith plagued my childhood, following me about, issuing orders and commands." Like an insect always buzzing in his ear, impervious to his attempts to wave her off.

"All of which you ignored?"

The corner of his mouth twitched. "Of course. Never was a boy so eager to leave for school."

"And on holidays?"

"It grew worse. After she pinned up her hair and dropped her hemline, there was a growing insistence that we marry without delay. I refused." Leo shoved a hand through his hair as he cast his mind back to the loud, unpleasant argument that had shaken the walls of the library.

"A woman's value is often calculated by counting her remaining fertile years." Lady Diana's words were quiet. "I'm quite familiar with the sentiment."

"Then came the war. Once I stated my intention to participate, to serve as an Army physician, the topic of marriage was quickly dropped."

"With the strong suspicion that she might find herself a young widow."

He nodded. "Absent my presence, I knew she'd wed another." And so she had. He balled a fist. "I miscalculated,

ANNE RENWICK

failed to account for her family's attachment to the land,
for the pressure that would come to bear upon my brother
to serve as my replacement."

Lady Diana nodded. "Edith married your younger
brother, took on the role of Lady of the Manor, and
promptly produced the presumptive heir—your namesake
and nephew—hoping all along that you would perish."

"A near thing on several occasions." He imagined Edith
had checked the lists of fallen soldiers regularly. "I did not,
much to my family's relief and her dismay."

"Why did you not return from the war?"

"There was much about the Crimean War I needed to
forget." And he'd known returning would thrust him back
into society's whirl, into events he could not yet stomach. "I
wandered, believing it best to leave my estate under my brother's care." Lost in his own gloom, searching for meaning, he'd
simply disappeared, leaving all to wonder if he still lived. "A
selfish mistake, as my absence denied my brother many of his
own opportunities." Including that of a happy marriage.

"Ten years after your departure, you reappear and
threaten to upend all her efforts. Then, late one All
Hallows' Eve..." She stood, frowning.

"What is it?"

"Twenty-three years." Her turn to pace. "You claim
consciousness of their passing, carve notches to mark
them, but not once have you been able to alter the final
outcome?"

"Not once." It was beyond frustrating. "My awareness
always fades as the evening progresses. I become lost in my
work, she arrives, begging me to reconsider marrying,

48

implying I ought not ruin my nephew's life by taking a bride. Not that I have pursued any of the single young ladies thrust into my presence by mothers eager to see them wed to a decorated war hero." He caught at the hem of Lady Diana's sleeve, stopping her before him. "But your arrival has brought me back to myself."

She shook her head, poked him in the chest and lifted her chin. "It's more than turning back time, or you wouldn't recall those years."

"More than," he agreed, staring down into the dark pools of her eyes, spellbound. Entranced. Bewitched. He'd spent years avoiding marriage, yet something about their souls called to each other, else why would the old yew tree grant her passage, but deny so many others? She was meant to be here. For him. And he for her. "I can't help but think that the alteration of events has something to do with you."

"Me?"

She was beautiful, his moon goddess. A touch brazen, stripping off wet garments with abandon before a strange man. If only the ghost of one. Save he wasn't anymore. For the first time on this particular night, he wasn't in a rush to bury himself in his work. He was more inclined to tug the crown from her head then, while her hair tumbled about her shoulders, gather her close.

An undertaking that, given the pulse that fluttered at her throat, might also interest her.

Instead, he stroked a fingertip down the side of her face, drawing a flush into her cheeks, basking in the smooth warmth of her skin.

"You're staring again," she said. Without backing away. Rising ever so slightly onto her toes.

"I would do more, if you'd permit a kiss?"

"Please."

A single word that might prove his undoing.

Sliding his hand behind her neck to cup the base of her skull, he drew her forward, allowing himself the sweet, agonizing tease that was the brush of her bosom against the breadth of his chest as he lowered his mouth to her lips. Pressing into their softness. It felt like a geological age, longer if he counted the years spent as a spirit, since he'd held a woman in his arms.

She tasted of autumn, of crisp apples, sweetly glazed and best consumed before a cozy fire as wood snapped and popped and tossed off bright sparks.

With a hint of innocent uncertainty, her lips parted. He was not gentleman enough not to take full advantage, stroking his tongue across them before deepening the kiss.

Her hands slipped between them, her fingers catching upon the buttons of his waistcoat. One by one, she popped them free with impatient jerking motions, until her palms could smooth across the linen of his shirt, exploring the width and breadth of his chest, the taper of his waist. Caresses that sent flames arcing through his body and turning him as hard as granite. He thrust his fingers into the hair knotted and twisted at the back of her head, scattering hairpins. Soft silk set in disarray.

Her crown clattered to the ground.

He ripped his mouth free to stare down at her, his breath coming in pants. "Tell me to stop, Diana."

Heaven help him, her eyes were dilated with passion.

As demon possessed as his inflamed body felt, he'd not press her for more than she would give willingly.

Her arms wrapped about his neck, pulling him back. "Not yet. More."

A deep ache demanded he comply, but not here. Not standing in the middle of the room with her balanced upon toe tips.

The divan? No, control would be too easily lost upon its surface. But the desk... Grasping her waist, he lifted his goddess, setting her—if not upon a pedestal—on his desk, scattering and crumpling papers and caring not one whit. Face to face, her hips level with his, he nibbled at her lips. Without breaking their kiss, he curled his fingers behind her knees urging them apart as a new hunger tore through him. Closer. He needed to be closer.

Wish granted, the smoking jacket fell open, exposing the curious bloomers that covered her thighs and the stark white stockings that stretched over her calves before plunging into ankle boots.

Swallowing a groan, he moved between her legs, filling the space. As hunger gnawed at him, he pulled her hips flush to his, rocking his insistent hardness against her soft center, enough to draw a gasp from the back of her throat.

He wanted her badly, but this was too much, too fast, too soon.

They needed to slow down.

He scattered kisses upon the corner of her mouth, down her neck and over the soft swells that rose above her corset. Where the amber pendant nestled between her lovely breasts, warm and glowing in the candlelight, much like the rest of her.

The small inclusion within had caught her eye, setting her on a path to Batcote Hall, to his workshop.

Slowly, and with great regret, he drew away, forcing his breath to an even measure.

"Leo?" She frowned. "Is something amiss?" Uncertainty and confusion colored her questions.

"Not at all." He met her eyes. "If anything, it's too right." He kissed her fingertips. "But we need to finish our conversation. Physical passion alone is not reason enough to indulge." He'd not rush blindly ahead. Better to step back, to consider the nature of the gift that fate presented, to be certain his own free will was not compromised. "If our time together is not limited to tonight, to a few private hours then…"

"I agree." Diana nodded, her face flushed. "We ought to sort out our situation."

"Zoological treasures led you to my side. What if we've a larger future together, one beyond this stone-walled chamber?" He waved at his crates. "Think of the discoveries we might make, how we might take the Zoological Society by storm. I believe our souls are intertwined, but to claim each other as husband and wife, we first need to prevent a murder." He glanced at the clock upon the wall. "And sand runs through the hourglass."

CHAPTER FIVE

*W*HATEVER HAD COME over them, Diana had no regrets. None.

Candlelight danced over the angles and planes of Leo's face, flickered in the dark pupils of his passionate eyes. He'd given her space to gather her thoughts. But only a little. The man was an arm's length away, close enough that his scent—wood smoke, soap and a hint of spice—still teased her senses. Wrapped in the surprising strength of his arms, pressed against the solid muscle of his chest, soft kisses had grown hard and demanding, melting her into a puddle of want and need.

Not at all like her experience with— No, the scoundrel's name had no place here.

She touched two fingers to her amber pendant. Like the snail within, she too had become trapped. Within society, yet shunned and suffocating, her only escape one of the mind. Without a life beyond her work, she was doomed to become one of her precious fossils, her academic papers the only trace of existence she left behind.

A future in the past with Leo?

Not relegated to the sidelines, not pitied for her lack of marital prospects. Not humored for an idiosyncratic shell-collecting habit that baffled and confused the *ton* matriarchs. Not a moldering old maid set upon the figurative shelf. Nor scorned as a forthright woman forcibly inserting herself into masculine pursuits, demanding her voice be heard. Here, in Leo's presence, she was an attractive woman with a zoological interest in snails. A woman intelligent enough to conduct her own research, to aid him in his own, to plot against a would-be murderess.

Tempting. Here, in 1862, was a man who was everything she could possibly want in a husband. World explorer, scientist, scholar, gentleman. One who hinted he would include her in his world, encourage her participation in academia, rather than relegate her to the traditional duties and functions of a wife.

But could she leave her sister, her mother behind? Or was that ahead? Would they miss her? Was it possible she might return to The Swan Inn this very same night, twenty-three years older, to present them with a most bizarre tale?

Diana shook her head, a futile attempt to clear her mind. There was no point in dwelling on what she might gain by lingering in the past. Trick of the mind or trick of the night, whatever this was, there was no hope of any relationship unless they prevented Leo's death.

"When exactly," she asked, sliding from the desktop

until solid stone met her boots, "must we be ready to counter this threat to your life?"

"If the pattern holds, Edith will arrive at a quarter till midnight."

"A little over two hours." No need to leave directly, then. "Do you have an idea how we might stop her?"

"Simple enough." The corner of Leo's mouth kicked up. "I don't turn away from her."

She twisted her lips, uncertain. There was a more direct solution. "Why not simply leave?"

A strange look crossed his face. "Unfinished business?" Hand at the small of her back, he steered her toward his workbench. "Every night upon my return to consciousness, I have a few moments of awareness, before I inescapably recommence the task I set out to accomplish this night, research Edith will later interrupt."

Inside the aquarium, he'd installed a series of glass plates to create a maze through which—and over and around—dozens of bioluminescent snails trekked, leaving behind silver trails as they crept toward their goal: a pint of frothy, yeasty ale. Already a few balanced on the rim of a German stein, sipping their rewards. Did snails sip?

"Snail herding?" She grinned. "Lured from one side to the other with alcoholic beverages?"

His answering laugh rumbled in his chest, a threatening new distraction. "I do. Ridiculous how much they enjoy a hearty brew at the end of their journey." Leo plucked a roaming snail from the wall, then pulled a glass rod from a beaker filled with a clear liquid and began to apply the liquid to the snail's muscular foot. "A dilute three percent sodium chloride solution encourages them to secrete a maximum amount of slime." He set the snail inside the glass box, where it hunched, assessing its new surroundings before setting out.

"You use the glass plates to collect the pedal mucus," Diana observed. "To what purpose?" Perplexed, she searched her mind, but could think of no medical reasons to collect snail slime other than to concoct a disgusting oral remedy for acute and chronic chest ailments and intestinal irritations.

"The purpose of this construct..." Eyes distant, Leo lifted the lid and set it to the side. He plucked one of the glass plates from its stand, using a metal spatula to scrape the slime into a glass beaker. "Are you aware that my function in the Crimean War was that of surgeon?"

"I was not. I'm afraid I dug no deeper than to hunt for information about the number of crates you carried home and where you might have hidden them away." She laid a hand upon his arm. "I understand the battles were horrific. I'm sorry for what you must have endured."

He gave a curt nod. "During my travels, I thought I'd put it behind me. Years passed, my collections grew. Then, on board a ship in the South China Sea, there was a boiler explosion. I stepped in to help, and it all came rushing back. Several of the crew members were badly burned." He swallowed. "Steam travels through the skin, burning deep layers of tissue. If enough surface area of a man's body is scalded, death is almost certain."

Diana clapped a hand to her mouth. An ache rose in her throat. It did not escape her mind that the future Lord Wraxall had, or would, suffer the very kind of burns his uncle described, assuming the linearity of time remained unchanged. Diana pressed two fingers to her temple, the parallels were almost too much to process.

"We did all we could—applying damp cotton gauze to the wounds, replacing bandages frequently, but it was not enough. Dehydration set in, followed by infection... Only two men survived." He set down the glass plate, reached for another. "Suffice it to say, my mind would not let the problem rest. Months later, I met a healer, one who listened to my story, then took me into the tangle of his garden and introduced me to this particular brown, blinking gastropod. This genus of *Asperitas* hails from Malaysia and is, to my knowledge, the only land snail known to produce biological light. But the bioluminescence was irrelevant. Snail slime, he claimed, was the best cure for a burn."

"And was he right?" She cast a dubious glance at the accumulating mucus, yet found herself mesmerized as he recounted the origins of his project.

He rocked a hand. "Snail mucin has agglutinant, adhesive properties and, to a degree, possesses antimicrobial properties. But on the whole, it is too thin, too watery, to successfully treat serious burns. What such patients require is a hydrogel, a thin, pliant sheet of material capable of keeping their wounds moist while allowing oxygen and water to pass freely through pores, a condition necessary to permit re-epithelialization of the skin."

Pensive, she tapped her lips. "When snails become more stationary, when they stop moving during dry weather, some species become immobile. They produce a thick, membranous slime that hardens into an epiphragm, gluing themselves in place until it rains."

"Precisely." A smile crept back onto his face. "Such a pleasure, conversing with a knowledgeable colleague. These past weeks, I've learned the secret is all in the chemical reaction. The trick is to trigger self-assembly of glyco-protein complexes in mucus to enhance adhesiveness when mixed with a supporting fibrous matrix comprised of collagen, gelatin, or chitin."

"I know little of chemistry." Impossible to bask in his approval when she knew she must share the story of how she'd arrived in his garden. On the off chance it held sway in deciding tonight's outcome, Leo needed to know what had happened to his nephew. But first, a final question. "And have you, with the array of equipment and chemicals before us, managed to fabricate a sheet of hydrogel?"

Leo tugged at his ear. "I'm close. Determining the precise amounts, the ratios for each component is proving a challenge." He lifted the beaker, peered at the contents, then poured the sticky, viscous mess into a funnel. One which ran the snail mucin through a series of tubes and filters, removing any impurities. He set down the glass. "Diana? What's wrong?"

"Your nephew." Her voice croaked. "The reason I snuck into your library in the dead of night is because it was the only way—and my sole opportunity—to hunt for your collection. The costume ball was cancelled. Your nephew, the current baron, was badly burned in a steam tractor accident." She swallowed, took a deep breath then, after sketching a bare-bones outline of her rivalry with Hector, informed him of what she'd overheard in the library.

For a long few minutes, Leo stared at his research, the corners of his mouth tugged down. When he finally spoke, his voice was a whisper. "Perhaps that is the purpose of our meeting. Not to alter my future, but that of my lineage. If, at the end of our time together, you return to your own time, hydrogels in hand, might you save him?"

"There's no way to know," she answered. "Perhaps it was the catalyst that led me to you."

"Is he married?"

"If you mean to ask if he has a direct heir, the answer is no."

He nodded. "Going forward, we'll consider both possibilities. Meaning we still need to address the unpleasant topic of how to stop Edith."

Frowning, she tipped her head. "Why not simply leave? The most obvious solution is to return to Batcote Hall and confront her in your brother's presence."

OUTSIDE, a bolt of lightning struck a distant tree, but the electricity seemed to sizzle down his spine. After so much time locked away, doomed to repeat the day of his demise, this might be his chance to alter the evening's outcome, yet he needed to face the possibility that doing so was to another's benefit, not his.

Curious how the future looped back to touch the past.

Regardless, to return Diana to the future with a treatment for his nephew, Leo needed to survive past midnight. And that involved stopping Edith.

He shook his head. "I've tried. Yes, even tonight, after your arrival in the chapel. I was unable to grasp the lever to

open the stairs, unable to climb them once you had."
Trapped as always, waiting for the inevitable.

Edith hated him. Hated that Leo intended to reclaim his
title, his land, and his manor. Nearly ten years of abandon-
ment, she'd screamed, ought to count for more.

But the papers declaring Lord Leopold Wraxall legally
dead had not been fully processed when his ship reached
London's docks, and his sudden resurrection had caused a
stir. Moreover, he had plans.

He'd spoken with old friends who were in the process
of founding a fledgling medical school, presenting them
with an outline of his research proposal. They'd been keen,
offered him a position but, quite rightly, pointed out he had
numerous personal affairs to set to rights on his estate
before settling in the city.

Not that he wished to delay his work with the snails,
hence his occupation of this space apart from the hall,
beneath the chapel, where he could escape the family
drama his unheralded return had produced.

While angry that Leo had sent not so much as a single
letter in seven years, his brother Marcus had welcomed
him home with open arms and introduced him to his son,
Leon. Long-standing tradition held that the heir to Batcote
Hall be named Leopold, a tradition Edith was quick to
modify, laying a tentative claim to her child's future, citing
the terrible toll of the Crimean War. But now, the worst
had not come to pass. There were opportunities Marcus
wished to pursue elsewhere, much to his wife's ire, and
Leo had promised him full financial support. It was only
fair that Marcus reap the profits of a decade's work upon
the estate.

"Show me," Diana said. "Perhaps the situation has since changed."

He lifted a foot, shifted his weight forward, but met resistance. Try as he might, he could not make shoe leather touch stone. Baffled, he stretched out a hand, and something with the smoothness of glass blocked his forward motion. Leo shook his head. "There's some kind of invisible barrier."

"There is?" She extended a hand before her, climbed three steps upward, and returned. All without meeting any obstacles. But when she caught up his hand, tugging him forward, neither of them could pass through.

"I don't understand." Diana glared at the steps.

"It must be that this is not quite the past, nor the future, but instead some liminal point in time. There is a certain resistance to our attempts to alter the timeline. How far will it extend? Does your freedom of movement mean my fate is already sealed?" A sobering and miserable thought. "For it appears you are free to return to your time, but I may not accompany you."

She crossed her arms. "I'm not leaving, not with your former fiancée sharpening her blade."

He snorted at the imagery. Dull or sharp, he couldn't recall. "Edith arrives at a quarter till midnight, hands buried in the folds of her skirts." A kitchen knife, he presumed, though he'd never glimpsed the weapon. Not that the specifics signified. Dead was dead. Unless you were a ghost, doomed to repeat the same night over and over. If there was any hope of escaping this endless loop, it was tonight. "Ostensibly, her presence would have been to oversee the opening of the chapel. A number of guests

61

expressed interest in viewing the working mechanisms of my grandfather's orrery-cum-armillary. But, knowing of the hidden workshop, she pays me a visit first. We argue, yet again, about my refusal to renounce my title, to let my nephew inherit. I turn away to attend to the polymerization process…"

"And she stabs you in the back."

He nodded. Through the intercostal space, nicking an artery and puncturing a lung. Not a quick death. His memories were blurry, but a vague impression of crawling up the stairs, of laying upon the chapel's cold flagstones as his life ebbed away remained.

But tonight, on this twenty-third iteration of his death, he would do his best to change the outcome.

"Did she close the stairs to the chapel?" Diana asked. "If so, we might leave them open, complicating—"

"No, I don't believe so," he interrupted. The hem of Edith's skirts disappeared, followed by silence—not clatter of gear or chains. "Better to close them, that we have more time to prepare." He reached for the lever. This time his fingers closed around the cold iron, triggering the mechanism when he pulled. Stones lifted and iron bars retracted into the wall. He stared at his hand. This proved what, exactly? "If this is neither the past nor a future, but some liminal point in time, we can't be sure of tonight's outcome. Will there be a resistance to an alteration in the timeline?"

"You believe our time together a stolen moment, a minor deviation that providence will snap back in place come dawn?" She frowned, annoyed that she could not bend time to her purpose. A strong-willed woman. Yet another of her attributes to admire.

"No proof exists either way." A numbness swept over him. To be so close to ending this torment of non-existence, to have finally met a woman with whom he could envision a future, to have aspirations, dreams and desires come rushing back only to be met with uncertainty and an inexplicable barricade.

Warm arms wrapped about his waist. "Divine intervention or a spiteful game played by fairies, if only a few hours were left to us, we must make the most of whatever this opportunity presents."

Gathering her close, Leo buried his face in the dark silk of her hair. Much as his body suggested the most pleasure might be achieved in a horizontal position upon his divan, he would begin as he meant to go on, beginning with a courtship in which he offered a lady a gift.

"Very well." Unwilling to dwell on the negative, he forced lightness into his words. "You came all this way from—"

"London," she supplied, if overly bright. An equal attempt to hide her concern.

"For my fossils and shells. I'll admit, I've not yet given them much attention. Shall we heft a crowbar and take a gander?"

She tossed him a half grin. "I thought you'd never offer."

With the stairwell closed, they inhabited a microcosm where all worries were suspended and the next hour was spent in happy companionship with conversation ranging across many topics as the answer to one question invariably led to a deep discussion.

The lid of one crate was pried free, then another. Each time, Diana exclaimed with delight, greedily snatching up the sheaves of notes detailing the contents within.

He left her to her gleeful explorations, inserting himself only to clarify particulars or to impart an amusing story of how he'd come to acquire a certain unusual fossil.

Her exclamations quickly descended into a happy chatter of paleontological minutiae that proved enlightening. He, a gentleman who had devoted much time to studying the natural sciences, appeared to have missed out on a number of scientific advances in recent—or future—years, medical, technological and philosophical. Bioluminescence harnessed to provide a biological light source—the sphere she carried an example of a safe, non-flammable portable light. The wonder that was long-distance air travel by dirigible. A man by the name of Charles Darwin who had upended biological studies by advancing the hypothesis of "modification with descent", causing an uproar in the zoological fossil-hunting community. The list was long.

Snail shells of all colors and sizes and patterns were arranged across his desk, all while she jotted down notes and observations, verbally outlining the numerous papers that must be written to bring his discoveries into the academic spotlight.

For his part, Leo continued preparations of the snail mucin cross-linking agents, measuring and weighing and mixing a number of constituents in different ratios. If sheer willpower could affect outcome, this All Hallows' Eve would mark the first successful polymerization into a solid three-dimensional structure that might be applied to the wounds of burn victims, preserving not only life, but permitting them to heal with a minimum of tissue damage.

He rubbed the back of his neck, trying not to brood over the meaning of his nephew's burns. If tonight failed to produce a new future for him, he hoped to preserve what he might of his lineage by sending sheets of hydrogel into the future with Diana, that his namesake might not depart the Earth any sooner than he absolutely must.

As the clock's minute hand made its final turn, as the hour drew closer to midnight, a noticeable pall fell over the room. Work slowed. Cheer became forced. He poured a final mucin preparation into its mold and set it aside. Already, a few mixtures had begun to take on a cloudy appearance, indicating the polymerization process was well underway. If—when—he survived past midnight, he might have a final formula for proposed wound-care hydrogel.

Turning down the flame of the alcohol burner that gently concentrated the latest batch of snail mucin, he looked up from his work.

Notes abandoned beside the shells upon his desk, Diana hefted a fire iron into her hands. The sleeves of his smoking jacket were rolled back so as not to catch upon this weapon of choice. Her hair was twisted and tightly pinned in place at the nape of her neck. Her feet were planted wide. His guardian, ready for battle. His heart squeezed.

"The goal is to prevent a murder, not to fill a coffin with a different body." His lips twitched. "Never fear, I will not turn my back."

Her hand wrapped about the amber pendant, thumb

worrying its surface. "You say that now, but if old patterns reassert, if your fate has been written and sealed—"

He held up a finger. "About that." Where was it, the letter he'd written earlier? There, beneath his notes. "Take this." He held out the paper, and she released the necklace, reaching. "Hide it wherever you think fitting, then 'discover' it. Later, you might present it to the current baron or whomever inherits. Claim the lost crates for your own studies."

Sadness stole across her features as she read his words. "Leo..." She swallowed, then cleared her throat. The dangling amber pendant shifted, and the tiny, coiled snail glinted within. "A note to the jeweler detailing provenance, offering him other pieces that might interest him while casually mentioning the location of all your specimens." A tear slid down her cheek as she tucked the note into her reticule. "Thank you."

Gears and chains clanked. Iron and stone scraped. The moment was upon them.

"Leopold," Edith called from above. "We must speak."

CHAPTER SIX

*E*XCITEMENT AND ANTICIPATION slammed Leo's heart against his ribs, but uncertainty and worry also pumped through his veins. Did freedom and a future await? Or would his actions here tonight only serve to aid his current heir, young Leon, now grown? Unclear. At the very least, the letter he'd penned would improve Diana's future, if only to stop that scoundrel Hector from laying claim to Lord Wraxall's collection.

He meant to challenge her presence from the start, but before he could stop himself, the same words he uttered every All Hallows' Eve fell from his lips. "There is nothing to discuss, Edith. The title remains mine. Your son is still heir. You may continue your reign as Lady of the Manor as I leave for London soon enough."

Fear pricked the fine hairs on the back of his neck, then wrapped its fist about his stomach with such force that it was reduced to a lump of coal.

"For now," Edith replied. "But what assurance have I that you will not marry?"

"None. In fact, you may be assured that I shall."

Undeterred, the hem of her blood-red skirt appeared. A suspiciously convenient hue. At tonight's ball, she was Queen of Hearts to her husband's King of Spades. For weeks, she'd fussed over their costumes. Coincidence, or had she been planning Leo's demise all along? His mistake, refusing to attend the event and announcing his intention to work through the night.

"Especially as he has just now proposed." Diana moved to stand beside him. "Please leave."

Tension collapsed. Her words and actions, yet again, broke past patterns. He clasped her hand, cheered by its strength and warmth, if a tad overwhelmed. Had he? Proposed? Not formally, though he'd made his intentions clear enough. He, who'd not given thought to taking a wife since he'd fled British shores ten—or was that thirty-three —years ago. Too many wished to choose a bride for him, a situation that carved a hollow in the pit of his stomach.

Until tonight. Diana's focused intensity called to him, instilling him with new energy and awakening a desire for closeness that he'd long thought dead.

Dead.

In her time, he was six feet under. But here, in 1862, fate dangled temptation before him all the while threatening to snatch it away.

A frisson ran through him, snapping his mind back to the immediate challenge they faced. What a nightmarish fairy tale this was, one without any assurance of a happy ending.

On the last step, Edith paused, eyes burning behind narrowed slits as the unwanted presence of a witness registered. "Leave? I think not. Not when my brother-in-law has entangled himself with a trollop."

"There is no need for such rudeness," he objected. Yet a woman wearing a man's robe, even atop a full set of undergarments, did present a certain... looseness.

Beside him, Diana's face paled at the accusation, her expression growing haunted. Did she regret their earlier intimacy, regret welcoming his embrace with such passion, regret permitting such intimate touch? A measure of doubt crept in. Ought he worry?

Edith shrugged, belittling his reprimand. A habit of hers, he recalled, dismissing everyone's opinion but her own. "A young, unchaperoned woman in a disheveled, half-dressed state cannot possibly lay claim to a pristine reputation when found alone with an unmarried man."

Edith's eyes swept the room, taking in the cozy fire, the multitude of candles that lit the space, then landed on the wet drape of Diana's spangled gown upon the back of a chair. "A quick tumble, young lady, is never an assurance of future vows. I ought to know." She jerked her chin at Leo. "He offers you nothing but empty promises. This so-called gentleman you think to bind yourself to ran off to war to avoid his responsibilities."

Leo's jaw fell slack as Diana sucked in a breath. Did she wonder if Edith's words held a grain of truth?

"Untrue," he barked, appalled that she would, once again, wield such a lie against him.

Had he been grateful for a reason to leave the family estate behind? Yes, most definitely. But only to avoid being trapped in the sticky web of lies Edith spun in an ill-considered maneuver designed to end in binding vows.

Though he'd badly miscalculated the depth of her resolve. Instead, Marcus had fallen prey to her machinations, a fact conveyed in a tattered letter sent to the front lines. Before it even had a chance to reach Leo, vows had been spoken.

"Is it not?" Edith replied. "Speculation has circulated for years about why Marcus and I were so quick to wed." Her gaze targeted Diana as, one by one, she let loose poison-tipped arrows. "I've a child who bears more than a passing resemblance to his uncle and all but shares his name. The golden hair of an angel instead of his father's pitch-black locks. Dimples, a certain angle to his jaw. His interests and pursuits and mannerisms those of his Uncle Leo. Traits that are very much remarked upon." She lifted a shoulder. "Society has reached its own conclusions. I have no need to confirm or deny."

"Lies," he growled. "I need only remind society how to count to ten, a number Marcus took note of himself." Leo squeezed Diana's hand and spoke to her. "There's a reason my brother refused her demands to have me declared dead, a reason he set solicitors upon my trail. No sooner had I donned a military uniform than Edith announced she was expecting, demanding an immediate wedding. I refused and left." During the argument that followed, he'd spoken words he deeply regretted, leaving Batcote Hall under a cloud of disapproval. That he'd later been proven right brought him no happiness for Marcus had been coerced into taking his brother's place at the altar. "My nephew was a small infant, born a full ten months past his parents' nuptials."

"People will believe what they wish to believe," Edith sneered. "Batcote Hall belongs more to me, to Marcus, than to you. For ten years, we've labored—"

"And I'll not evict you, my brother or my nephew from within its walls. Marcus wishes to remain here and my future lies in London." Or so he hoped. Could he convince her to turn around, to return to the ball without violence? "Why would you attempt to upend your son's world with such a lie? For what, a title?"

"There is much I would do to establish my son's rightful status as heir." At her sides, Edith's hands clenched. Neither held a knife. Not a weapon of any kind. He frowned, not yet daring to lower his guard. "And your trollop ought to know what she faces." The vengeful queen glared at Diana. "Leave. You've no future here. Run home to your father and pray your lover did not plant a child inside you."

"I will not." Diana dropped Leo's hand and stepped in front of him. "Your warped objectives, murderous as they are, cannot be allowed to stand."

Edith's eyes widened, and she took a step back. "How could you possibly—"

Crack!

Leo turned as the large flask he'd left above an alcohol burner shattered, launching sharp glass shards in all directions. Past patterns, ingrained within his neural network, reasserted themselves. With two long strides, he was halfway across the room, reaching for the cooling hydrogels as awareness crashed over him.

His doom was written in the stars, unalterable by the presence of a moon goddess. For a few hours, they'd managed to bend the linear path of time, distorting the past and defying the Fates. But the three goddesses now yanked the allotted thread of his life tight, measured its length, and reached with sharpened shears to snip it off.

Unable to turn, he grimaced, anticipating the sharp stab of pain. The sudden inability to draw breath. The cough that brought blood to his lips.

"Leo!"

At Diana's anguished cry, he half twisted, a final Herculean effort at rebellion.

The sharp point of a blade slashed into skin. Blood bloomed over the white of his shirt sleeve. Pain exploded across his arm.

My arm. Not his back.

Time slowed. Stretched. Then the frayed ends of twenty-three years spliced end to end snapped.

Hand clapped to the gash, he fell, landing hard upon the flagstone floor. The fire iron in Diana's hand whistled through the air, arcing to connect with Edith's legs.

She howled as her knees crumpled, as metal clattered to the ground.

"Leave!" Diana lifted her weapon above her head, her threat clear. "You'll be dealt with later."

"No one will believe you, a strumpet." Rage reddened Edith's face as she scrabbled across the floor. Agony contorted her features into a grimace as she struggled to stand. That she could walk at all was likely a testament to the layers of petticoats that supported the bell of her gown and protected her legs. There'd been considerable force behind Diana's swing.

"No one will believe a mad wife locked away in a tower room," she countered, stepping forward, sending Edith in a stumbling rush for the stairs. "But if you scream loud enough, long enough, perhaps tales might one day be told about the haunted Batcote Hall. A fitting legacy."

"Marcus would never." Brave words, given the worry that now stewed in her eyes.

"Are you so very certain?" Diana asked. "A woman willing to kill Lord Wraxall, war hero returned from his travels, a man her husband was unwilling to pronounce dead? No." She shook her head. "I doubt this evening ends well for you. You'll be lucky not to be sent away."

"This is my home!" Edith stood at an angle, bracing herself against the stone wall.

"You're no longer in charge." Diana narrowed her eyes. "And once I am Lady Wraxall, you will no longer be welcome within its walls. You," she repeated. "Not your son, not your husband."

Leo lifted his hand. Blood trickled downward across his wrist while crimson blood flowed from the gash, soaking white linen. But the wound was not a mortal injury. Stunned—if pleased—by Diana's announcement of their betrothal, he cleared his throat. "Imagine how Marcus will react when I present him with evidence of your violent tendencies. What gentleman would want to share adjoining chambers with the likes of you?"

She blanched.

"Leave," he ordered, with the confidence of a man embracing a new, promising future, "and contemplate what lies ahead. Ships sail for distant shores from Bristol Harbor with great regularity. Choose one. I expect your trunk to be missing by the time we return to the hall."

~

"HOW BADLY ARE YOU HURT?" Diana demanded, praying she wouldn't need run to Batcote Hall crying out for help.

With a great *thunk*, the stairwell closed above them.

"Alive." He blinked, glancing at his arm before offering her a tremulous smile. "And likely to remain so."

"You're bleeding," she pointed out. "Please tell me you keep medical supplies on hand."

He directed her to a battered leather bag. Within, she found a small bottle of ethyl alcohol, a roll of bandages, and a needle and thread.

Focusing upon Leo loosened the knot in her stomach, steadied her shaking hands. Not that she could so easily push aside the memory of the sickening crunch beneath the fire iron when it had connected with Edith's knees. How the woman had limped up the stairs, her face a contorted grimace. More than Edith's mind had broken this night.

Diana had braced herself for physical violence, expecting that words would fail them. How else to stop a murderess?

Still, when Edith descended, hands empty, Diana had dared to hope they might rewrite history. But the moment Leo became distracted, Edith had reached for the sharp, pointed spire of a sundial's gnomon—the part that cast the shadow of time—sitting upon the shelf among so many other broken and discarded items. Grasping it in her fist, she'd lifted the brass spire overhead, plunging it downward, aiming for Leo's back. Diana had screamed her warning and he had turned in time to avoid a fatal wound.

"The spire of a sundial?" He frowned at the bloody item that lay upon the floor. His words yanked her back to the situation, sweeping away the scrambled tangle of her thoughts.

"Indeed," Diana answered with a tremor in her voice. "A would-be murder weapon never anticipated. Lifted from a shelf, from among your grandfather's many abandoned projects." Her mind raced, struggling to place the familiar shape and design of the gnomon. Then the memory clicked into place. She'd seen it before… in the library cabinet that held a collection of astronomy equipment. Had Edith, in years past, seen the murder weapon cleaned, affixed to a dial plate and stored safely away where none would think to look?

She took a deep steadying breath. The shock from her own actions still reverberated. As Edith lifted her arm for another try, Diana had lashed out with the fire iron, connecting solidly with the woman's knee, dropping her to the floor, not hesitating at all to defend the man she—

Loved?

Her heart gave a great thud and she nodded, while her brain hissed, *too soon.*

Setting aside the gathered supplies, she offered him a hand. Leo rose easily enough onto his feet, reassuring— even if he did sink rather quickly into a chair and submit to her ministrations. Her hands shook as she pushed his waistcoat over his shoulders, unfastening a few key buttons to yank his shirttails free before dragging the entirety of his shirt over his head.

If the room felt a bit smaller, if her heartbeat skipped a beat when her eyes snagged on the defined cut of his muscled chest, it was only because she worried. Diana snatched up a nearby candle and held it close to his arm, blotting away the blood with the ruin of his shirt. "Not particularly deep." She gripped his bicep, maneuvering it under the light. Swallowing at the strength that rippled beneath her palm. They were near enough that she could feel the heat rising from his skin. "You're the doctor here. Your opinion?"

She stared at his generous lips, waiting for his answer while recalling their delicious pressure against the delicate skin of her throat and trying to suppress a rising surge of ill-timed arousal.

But no verbal reply was forthcoming. Instead, his hand slipped behind her neck, and he drew her close, claiming her lips with a kiss that began with lightheaded relief and overflowing gratitude—but ended with a warmth that spread outward, leaving her shivering with longing and desire. By rights, the rotations of the Earth about the sun ought never have let two souls such as theirs meet. But if this was a dream, she had no wish to awaken.

CHAPTER SEVEN

*B*LOOD TRICKLED ONTO her fingers, and she gasped, pulling away.

Ardent eyes bored into hers. "When the sun rises, we find you a room at the inn and examine our options for establishing who you might be in 1862, then proceed from there. We belong together."

"Or we walk out into the garden, together, and circle the old yew tree clockwise," Diana suggested. Could she let go of her sister and mother? If she failed to return, would her family forever wonder what became of her?

"If I'm *able* to leave this workshop, to step into the future," Leo frowned, "I'll have little to offer you as a husband. My title, my land, my rights—all are tied to my time."

"There is that." Economics could not be easily dismissed, though perhaps her soon-to-be brother-in-law might be of help. Unease crept into her stomach. Assuming the past had surrendered its grip, that the timeline now took an entirely different trajectory. Something to be tested and soon. "We've a few hours yet to reach a decision. First, let's attend to your arm."

Leo nodded, released her. "A stitch or two to hold it closed."

She blotted his arm with a ball of cotton drenched with enough ethyl alcohol that Leo hissed through his teeth. "Apologies. I wish to avoid any chance of infection. Now, keep a close eye on my stitches. I've darned a number of stockings, but this is my first time using a curved needle and this odd thread."

"Catgut," he corrected. "Made from sheep." A suggestion of laughter danced at the corners of his lips.

"Truly?" She grimaced at the suture materials in her hand, wondering if anything made from the intestines of an animal ought to be termed "thread". One stitch, then two. Both as small and as neat as she could manage. "Done."

But as Diana reached for a bandage, he held up a hand. "Wait. Let's avail ourselves of the opportunity to test a patch of hydrogel." Shirtless, Leo stood, sweeping her toward the workbench with a broad hand at the small of her waist.

Did he mean to spend the rest of the night bare to the waist? A proper lady would object, as Edith had so disagreeably pointed out. A flush crept up Diana's neck. No, she was no proper lady. Quite ruined. As there was no going back, was it so very wicked of her to wish to reap the benefits and admire the ripple and flow of muscle beneath skin? After all he presented a truly toe-curling view. With a swallow, she granted her peripheral vision permission to steal the occasional glance.

"Excellent," Leo said, lifting one mold after another, testing each with a gentle prod. More than one sample had solidified. "This one, I think." With a scalpel, he sliced through the hydrogel, then lifted a strip free with a narrow spatula. "If you'll play the nurse?"

"If this works," she laid the rubbery, opaque ribbon atop his wound, binding it in place with the roll of gauze, "you'll be the toast of the London medical community." Try as she might, her gaze kept slipping to the ridges and valleys of his abdomen.

As she tucked in the free end of the bandage, he stepped closer, then whispered in her ear. "We're alone. We've established the attraction is mutual. And I wish to make you my wife. There's no need to avert your eyes. Unless you'd rather I dress?"

"No." Her face caught fire as her heart tripped and stumbled. "Adventuring men do appear to possess much to admire."

"So long as you confine your explorations to this one man in particular," he lifted her hand, placed it against the firm warmth of his chest, "you might study whatever details you wish."

An offer never before extended. Her fingers ached to accept, an overwhelming desire echoed by every nerve in her body.

Diana slid her palm downward, over the ridges of his abdomen. So very, very tempting. And yet...

"I'm not..." she whispered, but stuttered to a halt. Neither was she accustomed to freely dispensing her charms.

Her experience of men encompassed a sum total of one.

Even so, her knowledge was spotty and incomplete. With the curtains drawn, moonlight hadn't illuminated much during their frenzied couplings. A certain amount of pain clouded memories of her first coupling. The second night had been better, thought he'd rather rushed—a touch here, another there—before sliding between her legs to bring himself to completion. Leaving her wanting... something.

She jerked her hand away, spun to stare into a candle's dancing flame. "I have a past. One that isn't erased by abandoning my own time."

"Hector," Leo concluded. His certainty rattled her effort at maintaining a calm demeanor. "What did the scoundrel do?"

To you. Words he left unspoken, but they were implied nonetheless.

He'd shattered her confidence, left her adrift in a sea of disapproval. "There was a country house party..." she began, annoyed at the tremor in her voice. "Passions were high and promises were made. Naïvely, I assumed we were to be married."

"You let him into your bed."

Accusation or a dry statement of fact?

She lifted her chin. "I did. Much to my everlasting regret. I soon learned my virginity was nothing more than a bargaining chip in a larger game. Another woman, two doors down from mine, we'll call her Miss Moneybags, was also played. Save she had a father willing and able to increase her wedding portion to such a degree that Hector could fashion himself a gentleman of leisure, free to spend his time in pursuit of esoteric scientific topics."

"Such as malacology?"

She nodded, wanting to look at him but afraid of what she might see in his eyes. "Not that he neglected his social connections. Hector is rather proud of the tactics he employs to claw his way up the social ladder. He took pains to share the details of my charms with a number of friends. Loudly and publicly."

"Leaving you?"

The truth was painful to confess. "A social outcast."

After Hector's betrayal, her already-small dowry was no longer sufficient to attract upstanding gentlemen. But the more dishonorable sort felt free to approach her. Men rather like Hector, who didn't hesitate to laugh about her gullibility. Over brandy. In their clubs. Within earshot of peers. Quietly, but persistently, the whispers had made their rounds until suitors stopped leaving calling cards with the steam butler of the Starr townhome.

Behind her, Leo moved about, no doubt dressing as he considered how to rescind his offer. Her stomach clenched, awaiting judgement.

"And so you set about to best him at his own game?"

Was that pride in his voice?

"In zoology, if not marriage. Turns out he's not as clever as he'd like everyone to believe." She dropped onto the settee, took a deep breath and held it as she lifted her gaze, surprised by the sight of his still-bare chest.

"A tale of revenge." There *was* pride in his voice. Acceptance where she least expected it. Her breaths came easier now. "Best served with a cold drink. Alas..." Smiling, he handed her a glass of tepid ale.

"Snail ale?" she sputtered, raising her eyebrows.

He laughed. "We stopped my murder, not an event that

occurs every All Hallows' Eve. A small celebration is in order, if not the one I'd hoped." He winked, then sipped from his glass.

Impossible not to watch his throat as he swallowed, not think what it might be like to kiss smooth skin where it met rough stubble. She shifted, rather regretting turning away from him, declining that alternative celebration he'd offered.

"Try it," he pressed. "I assure you, it was crafted for human consumption, not all for gastropods."

She sampled the beer, drank more deeply and found herself enjoying the bitter brew. "Quite good. Thank you."

His eyes danced as he sat beside her, setting her stomach aquiver. "So you extracted your vengeance by…"

"Reading every book on the topic I could find. Locating unstudied collections, hunting for specimens on every shoreline I could access. Then inserting myself into the zoological community and presenting papers on topics nearly identical to his. Save mine receive more praise and more citations. I've very much enjoyed the slow erosion of his status."

"Goaded by competition, you arrived at Batcote Hall, snuck into my library, and slipped through the hidden door and passageway to my workshop," he finished. "The first to find my lost treasure."

"Every step deliberate, save the last." She laughed. "But for an accidental encounter with *Illustrations of The Fossil Conchology of Great Britain and Ireland* by Thomas Brown—"

"Fate," he countered. "How many of us are ever offered the opportunity to turn back time?"

Time.

In that moment, it struck her. Here, in 1862, she had no publication history, no reputation of any kind. A clean slate and a chance to publish groundbreaking scientific papers long before Hector had graduated from Oxford. The thought sent a spiteful zing of pleasure dancing across her skin.

But was that fair play? Blocking Hector from entering the field was one thing, but to use her current knowledge in such a manner meant stealing the hard work of a number of scientists, even if they'd yet to assemble their data sets or put pen to paper to write the first sentence of their monographs.

Quite the moral conundrum.

Doubt pulled down the corners of her mouth. "I'm proud of my work but, our academic competition grows ever more spiteful." Edith's venomous acrimony held an uncomfortable mirror before her. "I don't want to become a woman like—"

"You're not," Leo said, shattering the sharp-edged image forming in her mind. His hand landed—heavy, solid and reassuring—upon her knee. "You're nothing like Edith. She shares more in common with Hector, lying and cheating, callously using others in the pursuit of her own goals."

"True," she agreed. "But—"

"Do you enjoy malacology?"

"Very much."

"Has anything suffered but his pride?"

"Only my standing in the eyes of the *ton*."

"Then there's your answer." Leo set aside his glass, took hers to set it on the floor beside his own.

"But it's not who I wish to be," she confessed. "A woman driven by resentment."

"Then stop factoring him into your decisions." He kissed the curve of her neck. The contour of her jaw. Her lips. "Reformulate your equations to include me and recalculate."

If only it could be so very simple.

Leo's fingers skimmed the edge of the smoking jacket. He slipped it over her right shoulder and began to explore the contours of her scapula, a brush of soft lips and rough stubble. The contrast was enough to curl the tips of her stocking-clad toes and steal the breath from her lungs.

"Leo," she breathed, dropping her hands upon his shoulders. "I—"

"Do you want me to stop?" His kisses slowed.

"No. Never that. Only my experience was not... entirely complete."

His hands stilled. "When that scoundrel slithered into your bedchamber to take his ease," he drew back, "did he make any attempts to bring you pleasure?" His eyes demanded the raw truth of her answer.

"Perfunctory ones at best?"

"Not at all the way to worship a moon goddess." The breadth of his hands spanned her corseted waist, drew her into his lap, turning her, her back pressed to his chest, her soft backside against the hard length of his erection. Corded arms folded about her, agile fingers fell upon the knotted sash at her waist. He nipped her neck. "If you'll permit a demonstration of the pleasures that ought to be yours?"

Though every nerve ending burst into fire, begging for

his touch, anticipation coiled most tightly at the tips of her breasts and between her thighs.

Refuse?

Impossible.

She dropped her head backward, resting it atop his shoulder. Reaching for his head, she pulled his mouth to her parted lips for a long, slow kiss. Then whispered the magic word. "Please."

LEO WASTED no time tugging the knot of the dressing gown free, pulling apart the two panels, and slipping it from her shoulders. Lust roared in his ears, urging him to make haste. He beat it down, refusing to give quarter—yet —to his own desires. Her pleasures took priority. Ones that bastard had denied to her.

If it was wicked of him to delight in that lack, so be it. He would be first to bring her to such a pinnacle and, if fate smiled upon him, the last.

Hands atop her corset, he cupped her breasts, thumbed the hard nubs of their tips through the satin.

She gasped, arching against him. "More," she breathed, encouraging liberties of a more intimate nature.

He'd not deny her anything.

His clumsy fingertips struggled with the fastenings of her corset. "Exhale," he ordered, his voice hoarse. She complied, giving him the room to make fast work of the steel busk, to release the cage about her torso. Triumphant, he yanked at the punishing garment, sliding it from beneath her and tossing it aside. Warm woman melted into him, molding to his hard frame with a satisfied sigh.

It was almost too much.

Aether help him, he could do this, even if her partially unwrapped state served only to stoke a smoldering fire that sent molten steel flowing through his veins and into his cock.

With her unbound, his palms slid easily beneath the thin muslin chemise, alternately gliding over smooth skin, plucking at the shadow of rosy peaks. He pinched one, eliciting a gasp. Her head tossed backward. "Oh! Yes!"

An erotic sight, to watch his hands orchestrate ecstasy, even if her every cry pushed him closer and closer to a cliff's edge. She'd fall first, but not before he propelled her to new heights.

Heavenly torture, the goal he'd set himself.

Of their own accord, her hips twitched, seeking more. Ignoring her groan of objection, Leo abandoned the tight buds of her nipples to slide his hands past her waist to find the slit of her drawers.

There, he stroked the tender skin of her inner thighs, urging them slightly apart, then danced his fingertips across the fine hairs at their apex before slipping inward in search of—

There it was. A welcoming feminine heat.

She jerked, clamping trembling thighs about his fingers, inhaling sharply.

Had that louse of a bounder wormed his way beneath her bedsheets, skipping over the very center of his partner's pleasure? So it seemed. He pitied the man's wife.

"Easy now," he whispered, gentling his teasing explorations, but not ceasing. He nipped at her throat, brought his free hand back to a breast to toy with its taut tip.

Once again, she turned to liquid in his arms.

"So very wet," he groaned softly into her ear, delighted. He pushed his iron-clad erection against the cleft of her arse. A promise of more to come. To him. To her. But not just yet. Later. First he'd see her reach her peak, cry out beneath his touch.

And she was so very close.

Her fingers gripped his thighs, digging in and holding tight, bracing for the ascent.

Stilling, he reassembled his focus.

Circling and swirling, he teased the engorged nub at her core until her breath hitched, until her thighs parted of their own accord in silent, weeping invitation. He slid deeper to press a single finger against her opening, seeking entrance.

"Leo," she gasped. Her hips jerked, welcoming the invasion.

Gritting his teeth against his own rising need, he pushed a second finger inward, stretching pliant flesh with a slow slide. In. Out. Over and over, only faster and with more insistence, grinding the base of his hand over her center.

Her hips rose and fell, setting an ever-faster pace. He wrapped an arm about her waist, pinning her in place, nudging his thigh between her legs, urging them further apart. Then he returned all attentions to the heart of her, to the nub at her core as her breath hitched and caught and scraped emerging as a strangled whimper.

"I think—" She twisted in his arms, arching.

"No thinking," he ordered.

Fists crumpled the wool of his trousers. She tensed in his arms, gasping. Then a delirious cry tore free from her throat as she came apart beneath his hands, soaring.

He gentled his touch to a barely-there caress as she rode the aftershocks back to Earth and settled into his arms against his chest.

Pride curved his lips. Satisfaction swelled with the knowledge of a goal skillfully attained. He forced his breaths to slow, urged his tense muscles to relax. Eager though his body may be, he wished to bask in his triumph, to rein in any untoward arrogance.

Though with each passing second, he was losing the struggle to convince himself an encore could wait a few minutes more.

CHAPTER EIGHT

*L*IMP. SATED. Delirious rapture.

"Aether," she breathed, collapsing in a wanton tangle of limbs and disarranged lace and muslin.

Slowly, Leo's hand stoked over her bare arm, the rise and fall of his chest even and slow. His motions soothing, his seeming languor betrayed for the lie it was by the dense rigidity that pulsed and throbbed against her backside, by the beat of his heart that hammered and thumped against his ribs.

Reminding her with every thud that this desire that sparked between them was far from gratified.

Anticipation pricked, prodding her own heart rate up a notch.

Experienced, she was not. But here, in this secluded location, surrounded by flickering candlelight, warmed by glowing coals, a boldness of a new kind reared its head. Sometimes the best and fastest way to acquire knowledge was by doing.

What touches, what caresses, what tweaks and pulls might drive him toward his own pinnacle?

A goal worthy of immediate attention.

She twisted in his arms, met his dark, molten gaze. The depth of heat in his eyes spoke of blast furnaces that carefully contained infernos reaching temperatures far greater than humans could survive.

"And?" His corded arm tightened about her.

She brushed her palm over the golden curls scattered across his chest. "Most wonderful." Circled a fingertip over the flat of a nipple, gratified by the sudden hitch of his breath.

"Do go on." Leo's mouth curved upward, at once both satisfied and hungry.

Quite impossible to resist.

Rolling, she brought their chests flush, pressed a kiss to his mouth. "Your explorations." She dragged her lips across rough stubble to the corner of his jaw, then nipped. "Were most marvelous. Revelatory. Life changing."

Time to return the favor. Ideas coalesced. And his smug look fell away as if he read her mind.

One knee at a time, hands braced against his shoulders, she rose over him, a determined seductress. Was she not, after all, wrapped only in the thinnest of undergarments? "Discovering your amber pendant in a London shop was the best thing that has ever happened to me. It led me to you."

Gently, he tapped the polished gem. "All set in motion by a tiny snail trapped in tree resin millions of years ago. Our moment was meant to be."

"And is not yet finished." She leaned forward. "For your

touch left behind a certain hollowness inside." What heights of torment might she push him to and how?

"I know a way to fix that." His fingers hooked over the lace-edged straps at her shoulders, but she swatted them away.

"My turn." She cocked an eyebrow. "Or would that be yours?"

"Ours," he suggested.

Broad hands caught at her hips, dropped them against his, then held them steady as he pushed upward. A rampant ridge of steel slotted against her soft, welcoming and most eager flesh, his trousers only a thin barrier between them.

Once rumors of her lost innocence wormed their way into the ears of certain ladies of the *ton*, lips had loosened in Diana's presence. Naughty words, phrases—indeed, entire conversations—no longer collapsed upon the arrival of a young, unmarried woman in the retiring rooms of balls, and she'd soon learned on one's back in a bed beneath covers was but a single positional approach to relations. Mentioned among them, riding astride.

Daring and practical. And exactly what she desired.

She stood, albeit on somewhat unsteady legs.

Leo rose onto his elbows, eyes alight.

Coyly, she unfastened the buttons of her combinations, slid the straps over her shoulders and let the garment fall. A slight wiggle of her hips was all it required to slither to the ground and pool about her ankles. She kicked it away, then reached for her garters.

"Leave them." Command and petition laced Leo's voice as he too rose. He toed off his shoes, then dropped his hands to his waistband and loosed the closure of his trousers. For a moment, dark wool hung on his hips, a mouthwatering sight. Then they too were gone. Cast aside by a burgeoning impatience.

One that rose, rampant, from among dark golden curls.

She let her gaze meander upward, inch by inch, slipping over the ridges of his abdomen, over valleys and planes of his chest.

"And?" He cocked an eyebrow. Daring her. No, encouraging her.

For too long, she'd been swept along in the currents and eddies shaped by society's expectations. Only when she'd stepped outside of those carefully drawn lines had she begun to understand, to appreciate the weight of the ridiculous responsibilities she'd been expected to bear—all for the benefit of others.

If not for Hector's betrayal, she never would have found her passion, a scientific calling, not to mention a mentor at the Natural History museum willing to take a young woman under his wing. Without hesitation, she'd jettisoned all hopes of marriage and a family, pretending no interest in either in a determined pursuit of scientific recognition. A goal now well within her reach, both in the future and here in the past.

But what of love?

Did that possibility stand before her here, now?

Aether, this was not the time for deep reflection, but a time to reclaim a piece of herself she'd lost years ago to the schemes of an individual unworthy of a single thought.

Time to shake loose the memory and redirect her destiny.

She pushed at Leo's chest, enjoying the command. "Sit."

He did. And stretched his muscled arms wide, resting them on the back of the settee. Waiting. Strong legs spread to accommodate the girth of his eager manhood.

So large. Bigger than... Diana shoved the thought away and climbed onto his lap, astride, settling upon his knees that she might give free rein to her hands. Careful to avoid his bandage, her palms began their exploration, learning his shape. The convex, the concave. The rough, the smooth. And all of him so very, very warm. Hot, really, as if steam coursed beneath his skin. Her restless fingertips slid over the hollow of his throat, behind his neck, and into his silken locks as she tugged his lips to hers, sealed their lips with a moan, and swept her tongue into his mouth. Strokes that tasted both bitter and sweet in a drunken revelry of ragged need.

Not once had she ever wanted any man as much as she desired Leo.

His broad hands fell upon her backside. Insistent, they resumed their own explorations, smoothing over her buttocks, tracing the outer curves of her hips. Then his fingers curled into her flesh, dragged her damp sex against his stiff heat. Need exploded. Closer, she wanted to be closer.

The tips of her breasts brushed over the crisp hairs upon his chest, sending a bolt of lightning straight to her core, turning her into a creature with but one need. To fill the emptiness between her legs that wept and throbbed with desire.

On a strangled sob, she tore her lips away. She rose up,

reaching for his thick length, bringing his crown to her opening. Then sank downward, inch by inch, welcoming the wonderful sensation of her passage stretching to accommodate his delightful girth, of becoming one with this man.

Full. Wondrously so.

Finally.

Rocking her hips to take him deeper yet, she gazed into Leo's eyes.

"Diana." A reverential, tormented groan. A brief moment of stillness before he erupted into motion, surging upward. Rising, falling, she met his every thrust with the drop of her hips. A mad and frenzied dance that pushed her to heights of inexplicable pleasure. His jaw clenched and his eyes glazed over as he pistoned into her. Her own body tightened, every nerve ending stretching, reaching.

"Again," he demanded, bracing his feet upon the floor to plunge deeper, slower and harder. "Come with me, fall with me, tip over the edge." He ground against her core, against that center of pleasure.

"Leo!" she screamed.

Sensation exploded, catapulting her to new heights of bliss as he buried himself inside her, shuddering and pulsing and crying out his own release.

They clung to each other, unwilling to part as their bodies cooled and conscious thought returned.

His hand smoothed across her lower back, passion spent and leaving behind something more profound. A glimmer of love. Theirs an impossible story, one that could never be told unless clad in the trappings of myths and legends.

Only glowing embers remained in the iron stove. A number of candles had guttered and died out. The small window set high in the wall still showcased darkness, though the storm had passed, but the clock mounted beside it informed her a few scant hours were left to them before dawn. Time in which monumental decisions must be reached.

"Stay with me," Leo murmured into the curve of her neck.

"I want to," Diana replied, pressing a kiss to his forehead. "But my heart is breaking at the thought of losing my sister, my mother."

"There's that." His eyes grew sad. "An inescapable and mournful loss."

"Then again, without my missteps..." No, Aurora was in love with her industrialist. Right or wrong, if society had not shunned the two sisters, the couple might never have met. To wish away their courtship was a different kind of injustice. Diana stood, reaching for her combinations. Pondering such deep complexities had sent a chill skating across her skin.

"You lose what academic acclaim you've won," he pointed out, pulling on his trousers. "Yet could publish earlier, faster."

"True." Her gaze flicked toward the pile of crates, traveled over the assortment of shells of current and fossilized species.

"Unless," he suggested, the corner of his mouth kicking up, "you find it too difficult to share the publications that will result from my treasure trove?"

"Never." She smiled at him.

Sharing. Partnership. Equal footing in the academic world.

Love and family.

All this awaited her in the past.

Silent, they dressed. After hours drying beside the stove, her spangled gown was only a touch damp. Diana draped the velvet smoking jacket over the back of the settee, smoothing her hand over its soft nap, fixing its memory in place, in case...

"Shall we attempt a walk in the garden?" They needed to test the timeline. To see if Leo would finally be granted the opportunity to leave the confinements of his workshop after so many years. She reached for her cape, frowning at the cobwebs clinging to the corners of the room. She'd missed them earlier. A trick of the light, no doubt. The guttering candles must have cast them into relief. As it had the dust on the shelving where the broken gadgetry lay.

"Yes. Only let me make a few notes first." A somewhat distracted reply, for all Leo's attention had fallen upon the experimental results laid out across his workbench. "I'll wrap the successful hydrogels to prevent desiccation, then..."

A vague nausea swirled in her stomach. Unsettled, she wanted nothing so much as a peaceful moonlight walk, arm in arm with the man she hoped to marry, to discuss how best to manage her appearance, a brief courtship, and a swift wedding before taking her place at Leo's side as Lady Wraxall.

Unnerving, to think that Edith might refuse to relinquish her position without yet another fight, but it must be planned for, expected.

Perhaps they might avoid some of the unpleasantness with an elopement. Could one still run for the border, marry at the Old Smithy in Gretna Green?

Diana turned, about to broach the subject, and found Leo staring at a snail pinched between his fingers, a deep frown carved into his face. "What's wrong? Is it your arm?"

HIS VERY OWN moon goddess was nothing short of a gift from the future. One he intended to claim with all due haste. In his years spent roaming the globe, he'd never met a woman like Diana. Passionate, driven and his intellectual match. For the first time, marriage no longer felt like an obligation to be endured, but instead the blessing so many claimed.

Impossible to suppress a smile, lighthearted and whole as he felt.

Holding her in his arms while he drove himself deep, fusing their bodies with molten heat, emptying into her while she shuddered and quaked about him—well, the very earth had shifted, tilted off axis, realigning their fortunes. He refused to believe otherwise.

Would it be so every time they joined together? Heavens, he hoped so. Hell, even now his cock stirred.

The moment the sun rose, he would arrange for a license, a minister and a brief ceremony. Then they would retire to his featherbed in the master chamber of Batcote Hall. In between bouts of earth-shattering lovemaking, they could sketch out plans to take the London scientific community by storm.

But first, a few moments of concentration to collect invaluable data. Amazing to realize he'd been so very, very close to success—had, in fact, achieved it. But for Diana's circuit about the old yew tree, he would not have lived long enough to record the outcome such that future scientists might replicate his work. Without her arrival, by the time anyone rediscovered his workshop whilst hunting for his shell and fossil collection, the hydrogels would have decayed and turned to dust.

Leo folded the waxed paper squares about the most successful hydrogels, scratching identifying notations onto the paper, then jotting down the correlating numbers into his notebook.

Done. He smiled down at the final blinking *Asperitas striata* to navigate the glass maze, a latecomer to the snail ale, only now trailing a glistening path up the side of the glass to join his friends. Only an inch or two remained before the snail hauled its coiled shell onto the rim.

Coiled shell.

He stared down at the creature's wholes.

Frowning, he scanned his workbench, plucked up a free-roaming snail. Then another. And yet another.

His stomach soured and churned.

Then the castle he'd constructed of starlight and moonbeams in the dark night's sky crashed to Earth.

"They've all sinistral curves to their shells," he said, setting down yet another snail. "Every last one."

"Uncommon, but not unheard of." Diana twisted her hair into a knot and pinned it back into place. "The majority of snail populations tend to exist in one state or the other, the better to align for mating. And the one I examined in the garden was sinistral."

"A single snail inspected after you'd begun your circuit of the yew tree." Leo shook his head. "Impossible to know if you lifted a variant, or if time had already begun to shift." Unease clawed at his stomach. "I distinctly remember recording the species as dextral." He set down the snail and began to flip through his notebook, searching for the record he'd made detailing their every character trait along with any and all variations therein. "Here." He pointed to an inked entry. "I surveyed over a thousand snails. All of them possessed a dextral conspiral coil."

Diana leaned forward, scanning this work, verifying the large sample size, all recorded in black and white. "Dextral." Next, she lifted a blinking snail, then another. She crossed the room, lifting a snail from the wall, another from a candlestick upon the mantle. Finally, she gave a slow nod and raised worried eyes to meet his. "All sinistral. But it makes no sense. Unless…"

"Time has not been set right?" His stomach flipped and quivered.

"No." She shook her head. "We righted an old wrong."

"Granting me time to complete my research."

"Unfinished business?" Her face blanched. "Is it possible we're not meant to…" Her voice, already a whisper, trailed off. She couldn't bring herself to say it aloud.

That the entire purpose was to save his nephew some twenty-three years from tonight.

Counterclockwise around the old yew tree to turn back time. That Diana might alter the trajectory of a night's events. Prevent a murder. Fall in love. Commit to a new and different future. But what if the stars in the night sky had only granted him a reprieve, a stay of execution. With the coming of the dawn would he fade into oblivion? Would a future sun rise upon his gravestone?

Frantic, he glanced about his workshop, taking in every last feature. He shuddered at the presence of cobwebs in corners and dust upon shelving, ethereal and insubstantial. They'd never been present, not in his time. Even with her present, he'd not been able to open the stairwell.

Blood hammered in his ears, an echo of iron nails being forged to fasten shut the lid of his coffin, as he ran to the lever. Only when his hands wrapped around cold metal, when the handle rotated upon its bearings, when gears turned, chains clanked and the stairs began to assemble could he finally exhale.

"Thank the heavens," he breathed. "I can still—" Leo collapsed onto the lowest step and dropped his face into his hands as a suppressed memory floated to the surface. "No, it doesn't matter. Everything has changed."

Memories, once vague, flooded back. The many iterations of past All Hallows' Eves had ended in a vastly different manner. In the past, he'd been left upon the floor, sharp metal stuck in his back, gasping for breath.

"What is different?" Diana dropped onto the stair beside him and caught up his hand, her voice frantic. "Was the mechanism jammed the first night you died?"

Miserable, he shook his head.

"Tell me." She squeezed his hand.

Tell her how he'd crawled across the stone pavers, his hands slipping and sliding in his own blood. How the stairs had tilted and shifted beneath his knees as he clawed his way upward, step by step, in the desperate hope that his brother would escort the first guests in predawn hours to the chapel before Leo drew his last breath. How blood had bubbled and seethed upon his lips as his world grayed and dimmed. How, for twenty-three years, he'd been condemned to repeat the experience, over and over, until the bright, shining light of her presence brought him a chance to finish his work, to fall in love.

No, such details would only increase her distress. Better for Diana to believe he'd died quickly and with little pain.

"Before tonight, Edith always left the stairwell open." He swallowed, finding it hard to share even the barest of details as her eyes brimmed with tears. "I managed to climb the stairs, but..."

"Then we go now, break another pattern." Diana stood and pulled back her shoulders. He'd seen that look upon many a soldier's face as they prepared to face battle. Focused. Refusing to acknowledge the near certainty of defeat. "If we make it into the garden, then we'll know there's a chance."

"For you, I will do my very best." Bracing a hand against the stone wall, he rose on wobbly legs. "But I insist upon a contingency plan. Gather up my notes. The ones detailing the origins of your amber pendant and my account of the *Asperitas striata,* from their discovery and classification to the unique properties of their mucin proteins and how they might best be applied to wound healing, to burns in partic-ular. Convey the medical information along with a jar of snails to the Duke of Avesbury in London. He will see the information falls into the right hands. But above all, do not forget the letter I wrote, that you might *discover* my collection in the future. Honor my memory. Publish everything and rise to greatness in the field."

The dam broke, and tears began to fall. "I refuse to concede defeat. There must be a way…"

"And if there isn't?" His fingertips traced over the curve of her cheek, struggling to find an inner calm, to accept what could not be altered. He tried to brush away the tears, but they flowed too freely now. "Then you must carry my love with you back to your time."

"While you hold tight to mine here and now." His goddess gave a tight nod, swallowed and dragged in a ragged breath. "This means your nephew—"

"Will be on his deathbed." Possibilities of a direct lineage were fading fast, but his namesake, his brother's son might yet carry on the name. "You'll take the hydrogels, do your best to save him?"

Diana nodded. She listened carefully to his precise instructions on how she ought to put the hydrogels to use, repeating his detailed instructions with precision.

"Now go. Put that oversized reticule of yours to good use." He dropped his hands to the flare of her hips, used the last of his fading strength to spin her about, to push her away. "Then we'll attempt a garden stroll."

As Diana bustled about gathering items, Leo squeezed his eyes shut, trying not to choke on a sudden upwelling of sorrow. Though there was no stabbing pain in his back, no gurgle of blood in his lungs, no earthly reason his strength ought ebb so fast, there was no denying that whatever reprieve time had granted him was at an end.

Step by step, he hauled himself upward.

He had no doubt he would reach the chapel, but he

doubted his feet would pass over the threshold. Save on the shoulders of pallbearers en route to his grave.

"Leo." Diana's voice shook. "There's a light bobbing in the distance, a lantern of sorts. Someone's approaching the garden gate. Did anyone reach your side before you..."

Died?

"No, not to my memory." The fine hairs on the back of his neck rose, for there was no chance of a rescue. Not with his life cooling in his veins.

What final trick did the fairies think to play?

CHAPTER NINE

*E*VERY CANDLE WAS SNUFFED. The fire doused. The hidden stairwell closed. There was only the chapel's door to be reached.

There, she would cry for help, risking the attention of whomever approached. Anything to save Leo. Diana could not bring herself to say farewell.

"Lean on me." She shifted the bulk of the bulging reticule fastened about her waist by its long satin cord, then drew Leo's arm across her shoulders, bracing her legs —but an almost insubstantial weight pressed down upon her.

Warning bells rang in her ears, but she refused to acknowledge them. One step, then another, she helped Leo shuffle toward their future. One they would share. Together.

Never mind the paling of his skin, the graying of his black trousers, the cooling of his body against hers. The night had grown colder and the moonlight filtering through the chapel's arched windows played tricks with the light. Once they reached Batcote Hall, everything would be fine. She all but dragged him across the threshold.

In the distance, the garden gate swung open, admitting two figures into the walled garden. She drew breath to call out. But lamplight illuminated a face, and the night air froze inside her lungs. "Hector?" Her question floated upon a shuddering breath.

Leo growled. "If only I possessed the strength to avenge you."

"But how can it possibly be?" Her heart began to race. Not help, but harm approached. And hiding within the chapel was not an option. "This is 1862."

"The veil between worlds is said to thin on the night of All Hallows' Eve when fairies and spirits are known to make mischief. But dawn approaches. Leave me. Hurry home, Diana, before you become trapped here in the past."

She blinked, shifted her gaze, ready to lodge an objection.

But beneath the starlight, the entirety of his form grew translucent, his features sketched only by thin outlines of no substance through which she could see bare branches and withered flowers. Like ashes through her fingers, he was slipping away.

"No!" She backed up, distressed to notice the heels of his shoes left no marks as she pulled him inside. And in the nick of time, for her grip on his arms faltered—no, passed through what was no longer flesh and blood—and he slumped to the ground. "Leo." Her voice was a mournful cry. "I can't... You were..."

"Fading," he finished. The rasp of his breath was like

wind through fallen leaves. "We're not meant to be. Not anymore. You must go on without me. Three times 'round the old yew tree, but clockwise." His hand reached out, passed through hers. "Run to my nephew's side. Do whatever you can for him."

Tears dripped from her chin as she sank down beside him to lean against the wall. She dug her fingers into the satin of her reticule, not at all comforted by the continued solidity of its contents. Nor buoyed by the hope represented by the hydrogels, monumental legacy though they might be.

"Diana, can you still hear me?"

"Every word," she whispered, struggling to focus as her world crumbled. Her love, dying, and she couldn't even offer him the slightest of physical comforts. Soon, her only option would be to continue bravely on. To salvage what she could of her future, alone.

"Sneak back into the house through the grotto," Leo continued, his eyes glassy. "The door will have locked behind you. There's a Green Man carved into the stone of the arch. Press the third stone to his left. Did you note the fork in the hidden passageway a few steps from the library entrance?"

She nodded.

"It leads to the master bedroom. Follow it to reach my nephew directly. You have your bioluminescent orb?"

She managed a watery smile. "And a jar of your snails. We'll find our way."

"Make me proud," he breathed, his form more suggestion than reality. "Go. Once dawn breaks, whatever sorcery imbues the tree with its magic may cease to work."

"I don't want to leave you..."

But he was gone. Vanished into thin air. Not even a suggestion of his presence remained.

Diana shoved herself onto her feet, spinning about, searching the shadows. "Leo?"

"Go now." Words not heard as much as felt, a soft caress across her skin. "Before it's too late."

Clutching her reticule and blinking back tears, Diana wrapped her cape about her, blotting out the spangles upon her gown, and pulled the hood low, unwilling to risk the chance Hector or his henchman might spot her past self.

Outside, an earthy scent hung in the night air, a reminder of the earlier rainstorm. She took a deep breath, hoping to ease the sorrow that tightened her chest, then darted out into the graveyard, weaving between headstones to reach the old yew tree without delay. Beneath the shelter of its widespread branches, she circled its trunk, clockwise. Once. Twice. Three times.

The fine hairs of her nape prickled as the air shimmered and the night's shadows shifted. Gone was the hint of damp and once again, the stars overhead shimmered in a cloudless night sky. Scattered throughout the garden were faint suggestions of yellow-green light, a glimmer of snails. And two new headstones.

Heart pounding, Diana snatched up a snail, then another, studying its coils through a blur of tears. Dextral conspirals, both of them. Time set right.

And yet so very wrong.

The crunch of boots upon gravel jolted her from melancholy and eased the constriction of her throat. There would be time to mourn later.

Setting the blinking snail back upon the ground, she turned to fix her eyes upon the distant, dark shape of the grotto. There was no direct path, no convenient tunnel of vegetation to lead her directly to its steps. She would need to zig, then zag, weaving her way through the garden to reach her escape route. Features lowering the odds of making a clean getaway. At least the ground was once again dry, mud no longer presented a hazard.

But Hector's greed would not be permitted to steal a man's life, not if his uncle's hydrogels might save him. Anger simmered, spurring her to action. Time to right an injustice.

Bent at the waist, arm wrapped about her precious cargo, Diana gathered the folds of her skirts in a fist, hauled in a deep breath, then darted forward, careful to move alongside the low hedgerow to hide her progress. The path twisted and turned—and spilled out into a small clearing surrounding a bubbling fountain.

"Stop!" A shout rang out. "You there!" A man took off running.

Kraken, they'd spotted her. Worse, his speed meant the positional advantage fell to him.

Altering her course, Diana bolted toward a dense evergreen thicket, scratching her hands. She snapped the satin cord of her reticule free from her waist and shoved it into the dense growth—all without slowing her steps. Onward she ran, her breath burning in her lungs, leading Hector's henchman away from the precious cargo, away from the grotto, heading instead for the open garden gate. If she could cross the threshold, step outside the confines of the wall, help might be within shouting distance.

Fifty feet, then twenty.

But the footfalls drew closer and closer. Harsh breaths met her ears. Then a thick, meaty hand closed about her upper arm, wrenching her from her flight, rendering her immobile in the space of a heartbeat.

Captured.

Two feet from freedom.

She kicked and thrashed, tried to bring the heel of her boot down upon the man's instep. But to no avail. The iron band of his arm wrapped about her waist and arms, slamming her against his rock-solid frame, no more pliable or considerate than a brick wall. Reduced to ineffective flails, Diana drew breath to scream.

"Much as I enjoy breaking pretty things, Mr. Godfrey thinks you might be useful." He slapped a grimy hand atop her mouth, clamping her chin in place lest she attempt to bite. "I take that to mean he wants you alive."

Diana froze. His was the brutish voice of the man in the library. The one who had turned Lord Wraxall's generosity against him, deliberately sabotaging the steam tractor.

She stomped down on his foot, but he merely laughed and dug his fingers deeper until she felt the bite of his fingernails.

"Well, well, well." Hector's voice sliced through the air like a serrated knife, reminding her of the many ways in which he'd shredded her reputation. The stark blue-white of lamplight illuminated the harsh planes of his face. "Miss Starr." He approached. Flinty eyes stared down at her, cold and assessing. "And here I'd thought our nighttime assignations were at an end. No need to ask what brings you here. You might be two steps ahead of me, but not for long.

Amazing how talkative that old butler grew once we offered him a little encouragement." His lips hooked into fiendish smile. "He pointed us to the gardener who was equally receptive. He directed us here. Seems there's a hidden workshop on site." He paused, letting his eyebrows drift upward in question.

Diana narrowed her eyes but stopped short of snarling.

"No need to bother denying it," Hector continued. "Instead, enlighten me as to how *you* knew," he waved a hand at the iron bars of the gate, "as to how you gained access." He lifted a finger. "But a warning. Scream, and I'll have George gag you."

"A knife to her throat would work better," George suggested. Malice and violence vibrated in his every word.

"We've discussed this." Hector pinned him with a look. "Excessive measures are not yet required." He tapped a pistol tucked into his waistband. "And if they are..."

Diana blinked. *Hector possessed a firearm?* Her will to fight vanished.

"Fine." The hand clapped to her face fell away accompanied by an irritated sigh.

"Answer the question, Diana." Hector's eyes bored into her. "With sunrise threatening, I'm rather at the end of my tether."

"When I arrived, the gate was open," she lied, relieved the mad dash for escape excused her pounding heart. "Someone locked it behind me. I've been trapped in here the better part of the night."

"Is that so." His eyes narrowed. He lifted an iron key. "The gardener swears he locks it before sundown every All

Hallows' Eve so as to forestall any nocturnal fairy mischief."

"How else would I gain entry?" Diana widened her eyes.

"Indeed, how else?"

"Please." Begging was a necessary humiliation, her only hope that he might extend her a modicum of mercy. "My mother and sister will miss me."

"But not until morning. Time enough for you to enlighten us as to your discoveries both in the library and in the chapel." He snapped his fingers, then turned on his heel, leading the way with lamplight. "Bring her."

Diana's feet were lifted from the ground. "There's nothing to be found!"

George ignored her kicks, tightening his arm about her ribs, squeezing precious air from her lungs as he hauled her behind Hector like so much luggage. She jerked her head backward with force, cracking her skull against her captor's jaw.

Quite satisfying, his grunt. Not so his retaliation.

Thick fingers stabbed into the knot of hair at her nape followed by a sharp jerk. "Enough." He snarled, baring yellow, rotten teeth. "Or I'll snap your neck and toss you behind a topiary."

"You wouldn't dare," she wheezed.

Hector heaved a long sigh. "I'm afraid he would, Diana. And, if you continue to be more trouble than you're worth, I can't say I'd be inclined to stop him. I might shoot you myself. Particularly after you've made every effort to destroy my reputation these past few years." He clucked his tongue. "George isn't one for hauling about dead weight, so if you'd like me to return you to your mother and sister unharmed…"

The tone of Hector's voice informed her he was deadly serious, and George had already proven himself overeager to do harm. She fell limp.

"Much better." A nasty light flared in Hector's eyes the moment before he turned on his heel to resume their march toward the chapel. "Here's how it's going to work." Orders delivered over his shoulder. "Cooperate, provide me with information of value, and I could be convinced to let you live, to deliver you back to The Swan Inn after our nighttime tryst."

A cold sweat broke out across her skin. A devious threat. Death. Or returned to her mother in a disheveled state, her gown ripped and torn. Society's tongues would wag. And only a few weeks before her sister's wedding. Worse, her chances of reaching Lord Wraxall's side, an undertaking fraught with enough difficulty before her capture, were fading quickly toward nonexistent.

This had to end. The bitterness between them had festered too long, poisoning every aspect of their lives.

"I'm sorry," she said.

That brought him up short. "For what?"

"For my part in all the professional nastiness that has passed between us. At first, all-consuming anger drove my interest in malacology, every publication was designed to take aim at your reputation." Acknowledging her role in this situation left a sour taste in her mouth. "It was wrong of me. But I've grown to love the field. I'd hoped to remove myself from the fray, to bury myself in work, far from the Zoological Society of London. A ceasefire if you will."

His eyes narrowed. "Extending an olive branch, are you?"

"I am." Though it was hard to hold a reasoned conversation while being carried like a sack of flour. They neared the stone chapel. "If Lord Wraxall's collection is so very important to you, I'll withdraw from the field. Only let me go."

"No." George's arm tightened about her. "She lies. Her tongue will wag."

"I'll admit I married the wrong woman." Hector frowned. "My wife's dowry has proven insufficient to sustain our lifestyle. You, a woman not adverse to tromping through fields or long hours in a dusty museum, have demonstrated a far better capacity for an economy of means." His voice took on a hard edge. "But our choices lead us ever further down a path from which there is no return. There's profit inside these stone walls. And my wife will endure a little scandal to keep herself in silk stockings and feathered hats."

"Profit?" Diana wheezed. "In crates full of fossilized shells? That's absurd."

"Found them dusty and worthless, did you?"

A trick question. Always a mistake, engaging in conversation with this slug of a man. "I found nothing." Her protest a final rasp of air. Stars began to gather at the edges of her vision, glimmering upon dark velvet.

Lantern aloft, Hector paused to scowl at his henchman. "For aether's sake, ease up. We can't interrogate a corpse."

The arm about her loosened, and she dragged in great gulps of air.

"Now, I happen to agree. Undocumented fossils provide

no scientific value, no matter how unique," he flicked the pendant that dangled about her neck, "and precious few items might interest a private collector. No, such is not the lure that ultimately drew me here. Mr. Rachet's secretary shared the oddest rumor about a medical treatment the baron pursued..."

Her stomach twisted. The secretary *had* known something. Dismissive of her entire gender, he'd declined to inform her, even when directly questioned. *The pillock.* If she survived this... "I have no idea what you're talking about."

"No?" His gaze, incredulous, snapped to hers. "Before Lord Leopold Wraxall died, he met with the board of directors in the process of organizing what would become the future Lister Institute. He was offered a research position to explore his findings in more depth. Something to do with snail mucin and medical cures. Quite the sought-after commodity. So you'll understand if I can't simply let you go."

Diana's stomach tied itself in a knot and sank to her knees. So much for Leo's work leaving no trace behind him. But for her mad race to eclipse Hector, to prove herself to the zoological community, this moment would never have arrived. How many would her professional pride injure? Lord Leon Wraxall lay on his deathbed. Her own life and reputation hung in the balance. And Leo's carefully documented discovery lay hidden inside a hedge.

Wretchedness borne of guilt and grief and righteous anger surged and seethed within her chest. "Merely yet another remedy for sore throats, aching stomachs and the like, I expect." Diana fought to keep a tremor out of her voice. Handing over Leo's notes wasn't an option. Along with the hydrogels, Hector would run to the highest bidder to line his coffers. No effort would be made on his part to correct any past wrongs.

"We shall see." Hector stopped before the chapel's door, snagged a snail from its lintel. "Bioluminescent. The only snail known to possess such a property and the very creature whispered about. By one turn or another, tonight will yield dividends." He studied it for a moment. "These curious blinking gastropods by themselves might prove a novelty. Imagine all the children who might beg their fathers for the novelty of possessing such a bedside light to chase away the shadowy threats?"

"Where they might shrivel and die of neglect?" she spat back. More life, however small, upon her conscience.

"Not my concern." With a shrug, he tossed aside the snail and stepped inside. There, he let out a low whistle. "Most impressive."

"After you, my lady." George released her, but plucked a blade from a hidden sheath and pointed it at her spine with a malevolent grin, daring her to do otherwise. "No sudden movements if you value your hide."

Deflated, Diana stepped inside. Dust and damp and cobwebs shrouded dark corners, lending the space a ghostly ambiance only enhanced by the flickering gleam of the candles Hector set alight.

Blinking snails dotted the ceiling and walls. They crept across the altar and over the rippling glass of the arched window. Not that Hector—self-professed malacological expert—paid them any attention. No, his attention fixed upon the unusual celestial orb suspended overhead. Assessing its market value, no doubt.

He turned about, gaping at the skeletonized brass rings of the heavens that hung above his head, at the mechanical gears and chains and counterweights, ready and waiting to set the stars and planets in motion.

"What an impossible mess of an orrery," Hector concluded, rolling his eyes. "Or is it an armillary? No, it's both at the same time. Or, rather, an attempt at doing so. Regardless, a colossal waste of time on the part of the builder, trying to reconcile a geocentric model of the universe with that of a heliocentric one. Worse, the contraption has been allowed to rust. Wasteful. Yet, while the planets consist of semi-precious stone, that gleaming sun is solid gold..." He tapped his chin. "But first things first." He rounded upon her with avarice in his glinting eyes. "How, Lady Diana, do we access a dead man's workshop?"

"You're standing in it," she replied. "Beneath a device constructed to observe the stars, to map the movements of the planets within the heavens. But since it's the snails you're after," she waved a hand, "they surround you. Is the bioluminescence not enough of a discovery?"

Hector drew close, baring his teeth in the facsimile of a smile. "Notes, Diana." His breath puffed, hot and fetid, against the skin of her face. "Though shells and fossils might prove a bonus."

She pulled back, wrinkling her nose. "You might speak with Lady Wraxall, ask for permission to search Batcote Hall's attics."

He sneered. "A button hidden among the contraption's

control panel, is it?"

Without waiting for or expecting confirmation, he turned away and crossed the room, holding the lantern aloft to study the panel of dials and levers and knobs affixed to the chapel's far wall.

Which meant his eyes were elsewhere when the air above the ancient altar shifted, bending light in manner that ought not be possible.

A shiver ran down her spine.

Was it possible?

The bowl of milk and honey rose, then hurtled through the air, upending the souring brew upon George, soaking the front of his shirt. A roasted nut followed, thunking against his forehead, then another. And another.

"Malevolent spirits are about," he hissed, as if the devil himself had materialized amidst the fire and brimstone of Hell's inner circle. A heartbeat later, his hand wrapped about her arm, and the sharp edge of his knife bit into her neck. "We need to leave," he called to Hector. "Return at dawn."

"No." Hector didn't so much as glance in their direction. "We finish this tonight."

An apple rose from the altar. It hung, suspended mid-air, then hurtled at the henchman's face.

George lashed out with his knife, slicing through the flesh of the apple, dropping its halves to the floor. He backed away, dragging her with him, blade once again at her throat. "Not if we leave them something to find in a distant ditch. Return unnoticed during the uproar."

The chapel door slammed closed.

Her heart fluttered. "Leo?" she whispered.

CHAPTER TEN

S TRONG EMOTION FUELED him, and the knife at his beloved's throat only served to drive him into a rage.

After Diana left the chapel, Leo had begun to drift about, formless. His consciousness fading, fragmenting. Then he'd heard her cry of distress.

Molecules had slammed back together, fusing into something neither spirit nor corporeal, landing in a space that was neither then nor now, yet still a plane of existence. One he was determined to occupy until Diana was well and truly safe.

The situation brewing before him was, alas, a tale as old as time. Two men, terrorizing a woman for their own gain. *His* woman. Unacceptable. The man with the knife was nothing but hired muscle. The other must be the insufferable Hector. The scoundrel who'd followed her to Somerset, arranged for his nephew Leon's accident without a shred of remorse and now, from the words that drifted past nonexistent ears, planned to offer up Leo's hard-won research into hydrogels to the highest bidder. Worse, Diana yet again served as Hector's means to an end, numbering among the disposable.

With the fury of a thousand incandescent flames, Leo swooped down upon them.

Easiest to grab them each by the throats in turn, until blood no longer coursed through veins and arteries, watching as life drained away.

Alas, his phantom hands passed through flesh.

A silent roar tore from his throat. Why permit his return, if only to render him powerless against this injustice?

Leo darted about, reaching, grasping, testing the boundaries that delineated his shadow-presence, noting his limits. He was confined to the chapel with no ability to manipulate that which belonged to the future. Otherwise, the blade pressed to Diana's back would even now be in his hands.

The past, however, was a different matter.

Thank heavens for the long-lived gardener with deeply ingrained superstitions who left offerings to fairies and wayward spirits in the same age-worn, hand-carved wooden bowls, year after year after year.

Leo hefted the bowl of milk and honey, upending its contents upon Hector's henchman, then pitched roasted nuts, thwacking the man in the forehead.

But his ghostly provocations only provoked entrenched determination and further spite. The intruders did not retreat. Diana remained a prisoner, the blade now held to her throat.

He threw an apple, darkly satisfied when the man struck out with the knife, if deeply troubled by its swift return to Diana's neck.

But the suggestion they toss her lifeless body into a ditch sealed their fate.

He slammed the chapel door closed. They'd not be taking Diana beyond his reach.

"Leo?" she whispered.

Suspended by steel cables, his grandfather's installation of the great celestial orbs and rings had hung in this chapel for the better part of a century, driving away worshipers while enticing astronomers. As his grandfather made attempts to correct the various misalignments and erroneous miscalculations borne of an impossible, forced marriage of Earth and sun centric systems, a convenient pulley arrangement had been installed, allowing for the contraption to be easily lowered and raised whenever adjustments were deemed necessary. In the end, the model had been pronounced "unworkable" and interest in the contents of an odd little chapel inside a walled garden had faded, and the apparatus was left to rust.

All but forgotten, save to serve as an occasional curiosity seldom put on display.

Which was to say that it was entirely plausible that the orb still functioned.

A possibility that Hector himself now tested, pistol tucked into his waistband as he bent over the control panel, flicking switches and pushing buttons, oblivious to the unnatural events that transpired behind his back.

This very night, twenty-three years past, the improbable orrery within an armillary had hung polished and shining, poised to provide guests with a pre-dawn demonstration of the struggles that had preceded modern astronomy. An event which had never come to pass because Edith had stabbed him in the back. By dint of sheer will, he'd crawled up those steps and flung himself into the chapel proper, out onto the floor where costumed guests, arriving for a heavenly display had, to their shock and horror, instead found the baron dead in a pool of his own blood.

Hadn't they?

No, that was wrong.

His mind twisted the repeating past with its most recent version. What, then, had killed him? Not the slice to his arm. Somehow the distortion of time had repaired itself, bending the brief divergence back into an inevitable continuity to ensure he did not walk upon Earth longer than his allotted time.

Was he truly dead? Doomed to another non-existence whereupon he would return to his forgotten workshop the very next All Hallows' Eve?

Not that such contemplations had any place in the current twist of conjoined realities.

He tipped his head back, studying the extensive clockwork mechanisms.

The drive springs were tight. Chains had been pulled and tugged until the counterweights hung near the rafters, then hooked in place. And never loosed.

A simple fact the frustrated Hector failed to discern, obsessed as he was upon the knobs and dials directly beneath his nose.

Dawn approached, and the revelers still gathered about

the dying embers of a bonfire would drift home. A plan formed. If he could raise a ruckus...

He reached out a hand, testing a hypothesis. Diana had been in his past. Could he? Yes! His fingers caught at a spangle stitched to the satin of her gown, shifting the folds of her skirt ever so slightly.

"Be silent, but be ready," he whispered into her ear.

Eyes wide, she gave a slight nod.

He drew a kind of breath, but that effort alone was draining. Best to conserve his stamina. Instead of wasting precious energy on respirations, Leo unhooked a counter-weight, the overlooked step to activating the astronomical instrument, then waited.

Eventually, Hector happened upon a combination of buttons and switches that set the orrery in motion.

A whirring sound filled the air as various gears engaged, then disengaged—a low and soft sound, forever shifting according to the carefully calculated, internal construction of the mechanism itself. Colorful planets traced their orbits about a golden sun—the yellow tiger's eye of Mercury, the blue lapis lazuli of Venus, the red carnelian of Mars—while mother-of-pearl satellite moons glimmered as the first morning rays of dawn angled through the chapel windows.

"It works!" Hector cried with a kind of glee, hand stroking his chin as he calculated the contraption's value.

"The offerings were rejected," George said. A tremor rattled through the henchman's voice. Not so his hand, which held the knife steadily against the delicate skin of Diana's throat. "We need to leave. Now."

"Or what?" Hector scoffed. He tore his eyes away from the orrery and returned to the control panel. "No. We're not leaving. Not without the notebook. Don't even think of abandoning me, or I'll turn you into the authorities. What's the penalty for killing a lord hereabouts?" The man yanked a random lever, turning the astrological brass ring in a different direction. "Which button, Diana? Or is it a dial?"

Leo gloated, leaving Hector to it. The grasping cur who thought nothing of harming others in his quest for riches made this almost too easy. A few more levers and opportunity would present itself.

"Such were your orders!" George cried.

"Incapacitate." Hector pulled a second lever and the Earth began to rotate on its axis. "Not kill. And what is a gentleman's word against your own, uneducated laborer that you are?"

A new anger burned in Leo's chest. Was it too late to save his nephew?

He lobbed another nut at the henchman.

"Stop!" Pale-faced, the man took a step backward, but without releasing Diana. "Fairies, you have the wrong man!"

Oh, Leo had the right man. Tamper with the equipment, arrange for a steam leak to burn his nephew, then attempt to steal the information while detaining the woman who might save him?

A second nut sent the henchman skittering sideways, and a third planted his feet exactly where Leo would have them.

He drifted over to Diana. Facing her, he focused his every thought upon taking form, mind concentrating his matter.

As he wavered into a half-existence in the present, her

breath caught. Love and longing filled her eyes.

"Shh," he warned, his voice a rasping whisper. "It's merely a matter of time. When the staircase opens, I'll throw another apple. Then we tip his balance."

The delicate tendons at her throat worked.

"Don't worry, I won't let you fall."

Leo peddled backward and snatched an apple from the altar, tossing it from hand to hand.

"It's only fairy mischief," the henchman reassured himself. But his knife hand drifted away from Diana's neck.

A moment later, gears turned, chains pulled, and the floor shifted, revealing the entryway to the hidden workspace below. Hector's hand had fallen upon the one lever he most desperately wished to find.

Leo's gaze locked upon hers. "Ready?"

Diana gave the slightest of nods.

He hurled the apple at the henchman's face with as much force as his incorporeal body could manage, a ghostly demonstration of wrath.

The man lashed out at the flying fruit, and Diana rammed her elbow into his stomach, twisting against his grip, shoving at his chest.

Leo ran forward, wrapping his arms about her waist and pulling her backward into the safety of his embrace, as the henchman's arms flew out, beating at empty air. A futile attempt at taking flight.

"AAAAHHHH!" Overbalanced on the edge of a gaping hole in the floor, he toppled backward. His cry was swallowed by the stairwell. Then abruptly cut off. A series of thuds followed as his body thumped and crashed downward over the stone stairs.

"What the hell, Diana?"

They turned to find Hector pointing his pistol at them. That is, at Diana. Whatever bullets were chambered within would pass through Leo's insubstantial body. Not an unexpected outcome, and one for which he'd accounted.

Momentary relief flashed once again to heated anger. Aiming a weapon at a defenseless woman? The vexation that was Hector had crossed a line.

"Stay calm. Lure him beneath the celestial orb, but do *not* join him," Leo rasped. "At any cost." He released her. One down, one to go.

Click. Whir. Moons and planets and star systems circled overhead, oblivious to their impending destruction.

"A ghost pushed him!" Diana flapped her hands, stumbling backward, leaning against the wall—a performance worthy of Drury Lane. She pointed at the black, gaping hole of the stairwell all while sliding her steps sideways, toward the door. "I think George might be... You need to help him."

"Why would you care?" Hector scoffed, utterly unconcerned for the welfare of his henchman. "First George spouts nonsense about fairies and malevolent spirits." He moved forward. "Now you wish me to believe that the long-dead Lord Leo Wraxall guards the entrance to his workshop?"

Oh, he did indeed.

"Who else would be so very determined to keep you, a lying, cheating murderer from discovering a priceless collection?"

"You." Hector stepped to the side, a predator blocking his prey's flight. "And I've killed no one. Yet." He waved his pistol and rolled his eyes. "But since you're so very concerned, head down the stairs. No sudden movements."

With one hand, Leo grasped the handle of the winch, using the last of his energy to hold it firmly in place. With his other hand, he unhooked the latch that locked down the thick cable. An entire universe hung in the balance.

Diana gasped, eyes on the overhead orb. "Is that—"

"Do not try to distract me." Hector took another step forward. "Move."

A single step more…

She shifted, ever so slowly. "But—"

Hector leapt forward, pointed the pistol at the ceiling and fired. The bullet pinged as it struck a brass ring, then clattered to the floor. "Move! Now!"

An action that burned any remaining qualms to ash. Leo released the handle of the winch. It reeled as the braided wire of the cable spun free, zinging through the grooved wheels of the various pulleys, yanked by the pull of Earth's gravity upon the fanciful solar system. The sun, the moon and the stars crashed down upon Hector in a hail of brass rings, metal balls and semi-precious gems.

Satisfying to see the reprobate sprawled, unconscious if still breathing, beneath the wreckage. But the warmth spreading through his body was more than a sense of triumph. A dim gray light seeped through the arched windows, marking the beginning of the night's end.

"Leo!" Diana skirted the debris, running to his side. She caught up his hand, pressed his palm to her face. "I believed you gone, or I would not have—"

"I was and will be," he interrupted, before she began to daydream of castles in the sky. "You're safe now." He could see her skin through his hand but could barely feel its softness.

"It's happening again." Her voice cracked. An echo of his own heart shattering.

"It is." He brushed his fingers across a soft strand of hair that twisted at her temple, then pressed a whisper of a kiss to her lips as molecules separated, diffused, drifted off in random directions.

"I love you," he breathed on a final exhale.

"And I you."

A RAY of sunlight broke through the window, and his form rippled, wavered, then dissolved into nothingness.

With the coming of the dawn, Leo was lost to her. In a single night she'd given her heart to a man who'd not only stimulated her mind, but her body. He'd wiped away past unpleasantness and, for the first time in years, she'd dared to dream of marriage, of a family, of a love that transcended time. Together, they'd confronted his fate, managed to bend time, to redirect its outcome. If only for a few hours.

Diana dashed the tears from her eyes and bit back a sob. As she'd traveled through time to save him, he'd returned to save her. But only one of them was permitted a future. A future in which she'd vowed to do her best to protect his bloodline, to save his nephew.

Hand pressed to the amber pendant, about the coiled shell within, she drew a deep breath. For him, she could do this.

Throwing open the chapel door, she gathered her skirts

into fists and took off at a sprint. Someone was bound to spy the open gate and investigate. With both her captors incapacitated, or worse, she could not be discovered within the garden walls. Not when a critical mission awaited her within Batcote Hall.

Retrieving her reticule from the shrubbery, Diana dashed to the grotto and found the Green Man carved into the archway. "Third to the left," she whispered, then pressed her hand to the moss-covered stone.

Nothing happened. Heart in her throat, she shoved. With a deep grinding and grating, the rock slid backward into a recess. The door's latch sprang free. Diana drew her bioluminescent ball from the depths of her bag and forged ahead into the dark tunnel, ignoring the dirt, dust and cobwebs. Grasping metal rungs, she climbed, then negotiated steep staircases that bent at odd angles, twisting and angling upward to the hidden hallway. There, at the fork, rather than turning right to reach the library, she directed her steps to the left, dragging her fingertips along the wall, searching for the door that led to the master suite.

There it was. A seam. A latch. An exit.

Diana pressed her ear against the door, listening. All was quiet.

But did that mean the room was empty? Or did the lord rest upon his bed, attended by a nurse?

No way but forward. She stuffed her bioluminescent light back into her reticule, then eased the door open.

The curtains were closed, the only light a dim Lucifer lamp that glowed upon a bedside table, casting a blue-white light across a man's face that only served to enhance the deathlike pallor of his skin.

The door closed behind her with a soft snick. On tiptoes, she stole to Lord Wraxall's bedside.

Astonished, Diana could only stare. Her chest grew tight and a heaviness weighted her heart, wrenching it downward into the pit of her churning stomach.

Save the difference of a few years and a slight bend to his nose, he *was* Leo.

They both possessed the same broad shoulders and long, muscular limbs that spoke of power. The same golden hair, if tousled and dampened by fever, spiked across his forehead. The same straight eyebrows, sharp cheekbones, and generous lips defined the contours of his face.

Every feature was drawn tight in a grimace of pain.

A gentleman laid low by the snake of a man Diana herself had led to his threshold.

She pressed a trembling hand to his forehead. Feverish. A weak pulse. And a rapid, shallow rise and fall of his chest. All worrisome.

Time to do her best to set it right.

She peeled back the covers. He was shirtless, his torso bare but for the gauzy bandages that covered the better part of one arm, extending across a portion of his neck and torso. A swollen hand sported an oozing bandage. Infection had taken hold. The situation was far worse than rumor had led her to expect. Aether, the pain of such extensive damage must be unimaginable. Would the hydrogels be enough to cover such substantial surface area? And what of the infection that threatened?

Interruption was bound to arrive in the form of a nurse, a doctor or, aether forbid, his mother. To that end, Diana needed to work swiftly and surely.

One by one, she set the paper-wrapped pliable sheets of polymerized mucin upon the dressing table beside an array of bandages and bottles—laudanum and a garlic tincture among them.

"Lord Wraxall," she called softly. "Can you hear me?"

No answer.

"I've a possible treatment for the burns." If not his fever.

She hated to do this, especially without the man's consent. But Leo had been adamant, and he was the physician. One intent upon saving his nephew.

Bracing herself for the worst, Diana brightened the lamp with a few shakes, then set about peeling away the bandages on Lord Wraxall's chest. Her stomach turned, then backed into a corner, cringing at the red, blistered, oozing skin she found beneath the gauzy cotton. Under her breath, she offered praise for opium, for not once did he stir.

Washing her hands with great care, she unwrapped the first hydrogel and placed it atop the angry skin. Again and again, until the worst damage was covered. Only then did she set about reapplying the bandages, grateful that he continued to sleep deeply.

At last, Diana sank into a beside chair, despondent.

If Lord Wraxall survived, he'd be scarred for life, but such was the least of his worries. He was entirely too still, too hot.

She slid her hand into his, gave a gentle squeeze, offering what little comfort she might.

CHAPTER ELEVEN

*H*IS EYES FLICKERED open, revealing irises the dark gray of a stormy sea, of an ocean that churned at unseen depths dragging long-forgotten creatures into the light.

"Do I know you?" he whispered, the timbre of his voice so very like Leo's that Diana's breath caught in her throat.

She swallowed. "We met once, years ago." At his blank look, she elaborated. "At a London ball."

Recognition flared. "You're Lady Diana, the woman Godfrey..."

Jilted? Abandoned? Cast aside in pursuit of fame and fortune?

"Yes," she answered simply, dropping his hand. How defeating to learn her reputation was so very tenacious. "I should go."

"Please don't." He closed his eyes. Long lashes feathered upon fevered cheeks. "I'd rather die with a beautiful goddess at my side."

ANNE RENWICK

His words, so like her Leo's, and yet... "Better you don't die at all."

"Such a simple thing." The corners of his lips turned upward, then flattened. "But the burns are extensive and," he half lifted his bandaged hand, "the cat trapped in my dressing room managed to express his indignation with a rather nasty bite. One now infected. Possibly the reason for my fever and chills. I sent to London for a Lister physician, but..."

Silence fell. Had he fallen back into a drug-induced sleep? If so, at least he escaped the pain.

Treating the superficial skin damage, as she'd feared, would not be enough to save the poor man.

"I'd meant to ask you to dance," he murmured. Not asleep, then. He drifted into past memories. "But with an assignment to distant shores, it seemed unfair to initiate a courtship. Then your letter arrived this fall. I made inquiries in the hopes that it might not be too late. A shame, my accident. I wish... well, at the very least, I'd hoped to join you in your hunt for my uncle's fossils and shells."

To dance? A courtship? To hunt for lost treasure? Diana's heart gave a great thump, but found it could not muster the energy to set a brisk pace. He was not her Leo, and it was too much to bear, the yearning. If she were to find love, perchance marriage, it would not be here at Batcote Hall.

"How is it you come to be here, Lady Diana?" His eyelids cracked open. "In my room? Not only was the ball cancelled, my mother would not have let an unfamiliar, unmarried woman sit in attendance. Not alone. And especially not one she did her best to strike from the guest list."

Lady Wraxall. Edith. Destined to despise each other before they'd ever met, be it 1862 or 1885.

"I..." Her gaze slipped sideways. The secret door blended seamlessly into the room's wooden paneling.

"From the library?" The furrow between his eyebrows deepened. So he did know about the hidden passageway. "No." His good arm stretched out, fingers plucking a leaf from her hair. "You've been to the garden. To see the snails. But how could you possibly—"

"It's a long story," she interrupted. One she could not risk repeating in detail, lest it find her assigned a padded room in an asylum. "A mutual acquaintance heard of your misfortune and thought you might benefit from a therapeutic hydrogel treatment he developed, one that has great promise in healing burns."

"And he sent you? Instead of coming himself?" His eyes narrowed, sensing her half-truth. "When this medical scientist must be near, otherwise you would not be the first to reach my side."

The moment the sun crested the garden wall during her final dash to the hidden grotto, Diana had felt the loss of not just Leo's body, but of his soul. Impossible to explain, as was her knowledge of anything remotely medical, let alone her grasp of groundbreaking biotechnology.

Her mistake, remaining at a baron's bedside when she ought to have fled, disappearing through the secret door to return to the library before scrambling down the ivy-covered wall and dashing to The Swan Inn before anyone discovered her missing.

But this was Leo's nephew, last of his line, and she found herself fixed to the seat.

Lord Wraxall frowned, awaiting her answer.

"Very near, but he is..." She swallowed the tearful lump that had gathered in her throat. "Indisposed." She drew the jar of blinking snails from her reticule and set it upon the bedside table. Impossible to explain how she arrived tonight with a treatment fabricated some twenty-three years in the past. "But he wanted you to know that new light shed upon your uncle's all-but forgotten work has enabled him to—"

The bedroom door swung open.

Leaning heavily upon a cane, Lady Wraxall—Edith—ushered in a white-haired man and a female assistant dressed in a nurse's uniform.

"Inconvenient, your countryside disasters," the physician chided, rushing to his patient's side, dropping a large bag upon a dressing table, yanking out bottles and bandages and a length of tubing.

"Siegfried." Tension drained from Lord Wraxall's face. "Thank you for coming."

"Of course. Infection complicated by severe burns, I'm told?"

The lord nodded, though his words grew slurred, he managed to recite a detailed account of his injuries and symptoms—two long-acquainted physicians conferring—while Dr. Siegfried monitored his pulse, took his temperature. "Varying lucidity. Severe pain. Fevered. Too fast a pulse. We'll have a look at your blood pressure in a moment, but..." The doctor shook his head. "Not good, Wraxall."

"I know." His words were faint. "You've the adrenal extract?"

"As requested." He lifted a glass vial. "Along with a sphygmomanometer to monitor your blood pressure." He filled the hypodermic syringe with a yellow liquid, then lifted bushy white eyebrows as he set it aside. "Both experimental, you'll recall."

"Experimental?" Lady Wraxall cried, distressed. "I'll have none of that!"

"Enough, Mother," her son chided, his voice weak. "It's not your choice." Surrendering his care to a trusted friend, he sank back into his pillows, turning back to his physician. "If—no, when—you've my permission."

"What's this?" Dr. Siegfried asked, lifting the baron's arm, pointing to his bandaged hand. "Only burns to the arm and torso were mentioned."

"A cat bite," Edith answered, dismissive. "Hardly a concern considering…"

She trailed off as the nurse and doctor exchanged a glance, then began to unwrap her son's hand. Red and swollen, streaks tracked up his arm from the bite wound.

"Infected," he pronounced. "And likely the proximate cause of sepsis." He cursed. "I'd expect circulatory shock and multi-organ failure are imminent. Though a saline drip might stave off dehydration, give you a fighting chance." Dr. Siegfried, a constant blur of motion, shoved a glass bottle filled with a clear liquid into the nurse's hands, one secured inside a metal cage fashioned with a hook. "Hang this. From the curtain rod if necessary."

As the physician shoved the lord's sleeve past his elbow and wrapped a length of rubber tubing about his upper arm, Edith's dour gaze fell upon the young woman at her son's side.

"Who authorized—" Edith staggered back, hand clutching the fall of lace at her throat. "You!"

"Me," Diana confirmed, rising from the bedside chair, baring her teeth in the facsimile of a smile. So very satisfying to witness a cold sweat break out across Edith's brow. "Here to attend your son upon his uncle's orders—in spite of your actions against him." If there was any justice to be found, Leo's efforts would work their magic, tip the balance of the scales to save his nephew. She clung to that thread of hope.

"Impossible," the lord's mother countered in a hoarse whisper. "You're nothing more than a figment of my imagination."

"Or your guilty conscience?" Diana suggested. "Presuming you possess one. I assure you I am quite real." She took a step in Edith's direction. "Did no one ever tell you a tale about an old yew tree beside a chapel?"

Edith's eyes darted to the jar of snails, and the blood drained from her face. "A fairy story meant for children."

"Is it?" Diana glowered. "Then how do you explain my presence? My persistent youth while the years have carved wrinkles into your skin and threaded silver through your hair?" Beneath a tiny snail trapped in amber, her heart—denied that which it most desired—cracked and bled. "Your attempt to stab your former fiancé in the back with the spire of a sundial might have succeeded but for the arc of a fire iron. Where is it, your weapon? Does it still lay upon the floor of a hidden workshop?"

"He still died." Claw-like, Lady Wraxall's fingers

gripped the silver cap of her cane. "So much for the magic of your enchanted tree." Despite her brave front, there was a certain shrillness to her voice that spoke of sleepless nights.

"No doubt you count your limp a small penalty to pay for years of continued freedom." Diana took another step forward. "Tell me, after he was found upon the chapel floor, were you the first suspect that came to mind? Did your husband ever surmise your villainy? Wearing the burden of such guilt."

Edith looked away, her lips pinched.

"Dr. Siegfried!" the nurse called. "He's seizing!"

Diana spun about, mouth open, frozen at the scene unfolding before her. Lord Leon Wraxall convulsed, his back arching, his eyes rolling back—all while foaming at the mouth.

Together, the doctor and nurse drew back the bedcovers, rolled the baron onto his side.

"I've got a thready pulse," the nurse said.

"Squeeze my hand, Wraxall," the doctor commanded as he bent over an odd contraption wrapped about Lord Wraxall's arm to consult a dial connected to an inflated rubber band. "Unresponsive. Blood pressure dropping." He pressed fingers to the lord's wrist. "Tachycardic. Pulse irregular and bounding."

"Convulsions abating," the nurse commented as Lord Wraxall's body relaxed.

Only then did Diana realize she'd forgotten to exhale.

But the calm was only momentary.

"He's stopped breathing!"

"I can't find a pulse."

Diana froze. Time stretched and warped as the lord's life hung in the balance.

Behind her, Edith dragged in a sharp breath. "What's happening?"

"Septic shock," the nurse answered. "We're losing him."

"Help me roll him onto his back," the doctor barked, frantic. "Start him on assisted respiration." As the nurse dropped a mask atop his face, rhythmically squeezing a bag, Dr. Siegfried began chest compressions. "It's not working."

He reached for the syringe loaded with adrenal extract. "You." His gaze skewered Diana. "Come. Hold him down."

Her?

Though her feet were leaden, Diana forced herself forward, raised shaking hands and pressed them to his shoulders. Heart pounding, she gulped at the slender length of the needle that flashed before her eyes. "If you can still hear me, Wraxall," the doctor muttered, "this is your moment." With steady hands, he positioned the needle's tip above his patient's chest, then pinned her with a look. "Hold him!"

Diana's breath froze in her lungs. Everything was happening so fast. He couldn't possibly intend to— Yes. Yes, it seemed he did.

"Through the fourth intercostal space and into the ventricular chamber." Dr. Siegfried plunged the sharp tip of the hypodermic needle into the lord's chest, into his heart, then depressed the plunger.

PAIN, both sharp and diffuse, shot through him.

Leo's back slammed down on the mattress, the feathers offering not an iota of comfort. Every vertebrae, every intervertebral disc protested the outrage perpetrated upon it by the sudden contraction of muscles, by the shock of so many arterioles contracting all at once.

Razor-edged and precipitous, consciousness rushed in to fill the vacuum of his scalded body.

His?

No, that wasn't quite right. He'd surrendered his some twenty-three years ago. Hadn't he?

Not in the least. Only yesterday he'd ridden atop the steam tractor, the winter rye finally sown, with nothing but evening festivities to host. His mind contemplating the possibilities a particular guest presented...

Then everything went wrong.

That much they agreed upon.

They?

All about, the air felt charged with electricity, suffused with ill-defined energy.

His eyes flew open. A woman gasped.

"Stay with me, Wraxall." A doctor yanked a needle from his chest, tossed it aside to smack at his cheek. "Give him room."

Air scraped into his lungs as a nurse lifted away a mask and the room came into sudden focus.

Who was this white-haired man, this physician whose intense, narrow gaze cataloged Leo's vitals? Dr. Siegfried, long-time friend and doctor, a corner of his mind answered. No, the man had been ever so much younger the last time they'd—

"Excellent." The physician checked a tube connected to a needle that pierced Leo's vein, then inflated a rubber band about his upper arm to consult an affixed dial.

Familiar devices, yet alien. A saline drip for rehydration. A sphygmomanometer to monitor his blood pressure.

How did he know such things? Because he was a physician and researcher at a prestigious medical school. Lister's emergency medical advancements were cutting edge. Except—

Bedside, a woman's face came into focus, offering him water.

"Diana," he whispered, suffused with happiness. She'd made it back to his room. Grateful, he sipped from the cup. "You applied the hydrogels to my burns. Thank you."

"Leo?" she breathed on a shaky exhale. Astonished, she bent close. "Yes, all but two. But how can it be?"

"Two," he murmured. "The damage was that extensive? We might need mucin. You've the jar of snails still? Returning to the workshop probably not an option, considering—"

"Shh." Diana pressed a finger to his lips. "Not now."

"Much improved," Dr. Siegfried pronounced, confused. "Your fever appears to have broken, though such a swift recovery is near impossible given..." He trailed off, frowning. "The buzzards still circle, but you'll live to fight another day. Let's have a look at the burn wounds, shall we?" He peeled back a patch of gauze and hesitated. "What's this?"

"Hydrogels," Diana answered. "A new method to treat wounds and severe burns. Possessing mild antimicrobial activity, the flexible material seals the wound and allows for gas exchange while maintaining hydration levels."

Pride swelled in his chest.

"Wraxall." The doctor frowned. "You authorized this?"

"More than that," he murmured, annoyed at the fever that slowed his mind, weighted his words. "Designed it. Polymerized snail mucin…"

"Snail?" Dr. Siegfried's eyebrows climbed up his forehead. "As in gastropods?"

"Indeed."

"What's the fuss?" A cane thumped heavily upon the floor. "Is my son—" Edith's face loomed above him. "What happened to your eyes?"

He met the woman's gaze. "Are they so very different?"

"No." His mother—Edith—glared down at him. "It can't be. My son—"

"Is exceedingly distressed to learn of his mother's treachery." Sympathy for her plight Leo could manage, if not empathy. After his father's death, much of his upbringing had been miserable. School—Eton—had been a welcome escape.

"You've stolen my son." Edith's mouth opened. Closed. She glanced at Diana, then back to him. "Return him." A command that emerged strangely slurred.

"Lady Wraxall?" Dr. Siegfried laid a hand upon her arm.

Edith stiffened. The left side of her face drooped. Her cane clattered to the floor. She sagged, collapsing onto the ground, burbling unintelligible words, in a pool of mauve silk.

Muttering under his breath, the physician bent to take her pulse. "We've a new patient," he informed the nurse on a heavy sigh. "Suspected apoplexy. She's in need of a bed. You," he pointed at Diana, "stay here. Watch him."

Activity exploded. In short order, a strange, wheeled contraption Leo somehow knew to be a steambot was summoned, and Edith, Lady of the Manor, was borne away to a room of her own.

Leaving him alone with Diana and the possibility of a curious new future.

"My eyes?" he asked.

"STILL BLUE." Heart pounding, knees weak, Diana lowered herself onto the edge of the mattress, sweeping up his hand to press his palm to her cheek. "But neither a deep sapphire nor a steely gray. Instead, a brilliant azure." Simple, factual words whispered while euphoria hummed though her, tipping her world off balance once more. "The sun rose and my heart broke. You were gone. How —?" Overwhelmed, astonished, yet trembling with happiness, she couldn't frame the right question. "I don't understand. What happened? What of the current baron?"

"It's me, your Leo. But also my nephew, a man who has lived—lives—a most interesting life. I can't quite explain, but we've…"

"Blended?" Disbelief tingled in her chest. *How could this be?*

"Merged. I've both my memories and his memories. Separate yet of one sound mind." The corner of his mouth lifted. "When the doctor brought him back from the verge of death, minutes ago, my consciousness somehow slipped inside to join his own."

"Then he—you—know that this," she waved a trembling hand over his bandages, "the accident, is partly my fault. I led Hector here. Even now, he and his henchman, George, lie in the chapel…"

"Godfrey is badly injured, but not dead." Leo struggled to sit upright. Diana assisted, tucking a number of pillows behind his back. "Though it would serve him right if he was. He was still breathing when I… departed. His henchman, on the other hand, has paid the ultimate price for attempted murder and is no longer a problem." He exhaled, a long, drawn-out sigh. "I will, of course, need to contact the authorities, but any blame sits squarely on their shoulders. Misadventure while trespassing to commit a crime."

"Hector will tell tales," she warned.

"Of a ghost haunting my family's chapel?" Leo grinned, then shrugged. "Who will believe him? He'll be written off as a madman and dismissed as credible zoologist."

A point that would have been more satisfying were her own behavior above reproach. "And what of my role, did—does—the part of you that is Leon not harbor suspicion?"

"You are not in the least responsible." Leo squeezed her hand. "Godfrey, unscrupulous treasure hunter, is to blame. He chose to associate with questionable characters, with individuals known for trafficking unproven medical cures to the highest bidder. When he expressed an interest in visiting Batcote Hall, I sent him an invitation, then contacted my employer."

"And my letter begging an audience?"

"Also flagged as suspicious."

Her stomach sank. "And now I've been caught, red-handed, sneaking all about your property."

"Diana, my love, you never intended to steal anything. If anything, you sought to save a piece of lost history." He stroked a finger down the side of her face. "I spent days planning to whirl you across the ballroom floor, to ply you with champagne and tease the truth from you, hoping that the woman I met all those years ago might still spark my interest. That I, and not just my zoological collection, tempts you."

Acceptance came gradually, but not without much effort to drive away lingering doubt. There was no logical explanation, no scientific reason to explain the presence of Leo's soul now residing in his nephew's body. But after what she'd witnessed, experienced this past night...

"It would have worked," she whispered, brushing aside a golden lock. Different from her memory only in its length. "Instead, an accident."

"And a fairy-tale romance," he finished. "One with a happy ending. My fever," he lifted her hand to his forehead, "is already gone. The pain, half what it was. Perhaps, after last night's events, we ought to know better than to question the forces determined to bring us together."

"Meaning?"

"Stay. Let me send for your mother and sister. We'll make a new beginning, one wherein I court you properly."

"Properly?" She lifted her eyebrows. "How very disappointing."

Lust flared in his eyes. "Improperly, then. But only once you agree to wear my ring and a date is set, and soon."

"Long walks in a certain garden beneath the sun and the moon?"

"Beneath all the planets," he promised. "We'll see the chapel restored, our workshop reclaimed for when we visit Somerset."

"I'd like that." Her heart soared. Then dropped. "What of Edith?"

"We'll leave her the house, shall we not? Ivy-covered stone walls and land always ranked above me, above family. Let her continue as Lady of the Manor, our place is elsewhere. Your work, my work, the Natural History Museum, the Lister Institute—both our immediate futures are based in London. From there, we'll travel to distant shores in search of the most interesting gastropods to share with the world." Smiling, he kissed her fingers, then slid a golden signet ring from his hand onto her thumb.

Her eyes grew teary, this time from joy. "Is that a proposal?"

It ought not be possible, the manner in which this fall, cross-quarter night had brought love into her life, a man who wanted her for herself. She blinked back tears at the sight of Leo's ring upon her hand. Against all odds, she would walk among the *ton*, her respectability restored.

"It is." His eyes glittered. "I, Lord Leo Wraxall, both past and present, want you in my life for evermore. Will you marry me?"

"Yes," she whispered, "of course I will." A heartbeat later, their lips met.

Everything else was spoken without exchanging a single word.

EPILOGUE

O N THE EVENING of the winter solstice, they married in candlelight. Beneath the whirling circles of the heavens and the revolving orbits of planets. In the presence of family—her mother, her newlywed sister and brother-in-law—along with a few close friends from the Lister Institute and the Natural History Museum. And a handful of blinking snails.

Pride of place belonged to Diana's mother. Seated upon the front pew, she beamed. In moments, both her daughters would be married—love matches, no less—and to men who occupied favorable positions in society. No longer would her friends sigh softly and shake their heads.

Absent was Edith. For, though having lost the use of her left side and the ability to speak clearly, her objection to attending the ceremony had been vehement and clear. She remained behind in the hall under the care of her nurse.

Diana stood before the ancient altar, a glowing amber

149

pendant about her throat and a somewhat tarnished celestial crown upon her head—one mysteriously found within the forgotten workshop beneath their feet. Leo, wounds healed with a minimum of scarring, held her hands. In turn, they voiced age-old vows, binding themselves to each other once and for all.

ELEMENTAL STEAMPUNK

Keep Reading for the opening chapters of
THE GOLDEN SPIDER

THE GOLDEN SPIDER

AN ELEMENTAL STEAMPUNK CHRONICLE –
BOOK ONE

A stolen clockwork spider.
A forbidden romance.
A murderous spy on the streets of London who must be stopped
before it's too late.

CHAPTER ONE

London, Fall 1884

*T*HE HONOR OF WORKING for the Queen as a
spy was overrated.

Crouched behind a burned-out steam carriage, Sebastian Talbot, the 5th Earl of Thornton, tapped on the acousticocept wrapped about his ear. The device should have worked up to a half-mile distance. He squinted through the gloom of the riverside fog. Hell, he could still see their agent. He just couldn't hear him.

"No signal," he hissed to the man beside him. Would they ever manage to make this damn device work in the field?

His partner, Mr. Black, frowned. "Same."

"Repairs." Thornton pointed across the field of rusting scrap metal before them to a derelict water boiler just large enough to conceal both men in the dark of night. "There."

After years of working side by side, the two men could almost read each other's minds.

Black nodded and they ran forward, tracing a winding path through piles of discarded machinery in an attempt to melt into the odd shadows the metal cast. Their agent was no more than fifty feet away, but Thornton still couldn't hear the conversation between Agent Smith and his informant. He threw Black a questioning look, but the man shook his head. Nothing.

Thornton bit back a curse. They couldn't approach Smith without blowing his cover.

Black ripped the acousticocept from his ear and twisted its dials in vain trying to increase reception. The light continued to blink red. Either the agent's artificial ear had failed or there was some fresh blunder with the receiver.

Thornton ran through the schematics in his mind. The aether chamber inside the agent's ear was sealed. Tests had proven that in the laboratory this afternoon. The next logical weak point was the needles contacting the counter rotating disks in the acousticocepts. They had a tendency to dislodge.

He wanted to growl in frustration. Henri should have fixed that problem by now. The device should be beyond field trials. They should have been sitting in a steam coach listening to the informant's tale in complete warmth and comfort, not running about a scrap yard straight from a debriefing at the opera and risking discovery in blindingly white shirts, snowy cravats, and well-tailored coats. Thornton kept a hand tightly wrapped over his silver-capped cane lest it reflect some stray ray of light and draw attention like a bioluminescent beacon.

And his leg was sending out pangs of warning. Damn sky pirate and his cutlass.

Thornton ignored the radiating pain. He pulled a cigarette case from his coat pocket as he stepped behind the metal tank. He raised his eyebrows at Black. Smith believed his informant finally had a solid lead. If Thornton didn't attempt field repairs, he and Black would be reduced to simple observation. Too many carefully woven plans had unraveled of late, and he did not relish the thought of delivering yet another report of failure to his superior.

Black nodded and angled his torso to further block any view of Thornton's activities. Flipping it open, he activated the small decilamp—its light a necessary risk—and selected micro-tweezers from among the various tools within. There was a chance he could reset the needles of the acousticocept before the agent moved to follow the informant's lead.

His cold fingers fumbled. Gloves. He'd been about to return for them when he'd spotted a determined mother steering her debutant daughter into his opera box. Discomfort, no matter how biting, was preferable to becoming trapped in such a snare. Warmth had been abandoned in favor of freedom.

Black shifted closer as Thornton pulled his acousticocept free and placed it on a steam gauge protruding from the boiler. Thornton flipped a monocle over his eye and, with only the faint blue-green light to illuminate the needles, set to work.

As always, the world about him faded as he untangled an experimental conundrum.

Moments later, the light glowed a steady green. Success,

but no satisfaction. He'd uncovered yet another internal defect. Tomorrow, he would sketch out modifications to solve this issue once and for all. He handed the device to Black and set about fixing the second one. Hooking the working acousticocept once again about his ear, Thornton was drawn into the distant exchange.

"...but how is the eye doctor making contact with the gypsies?" Smith asked.

The ragged informant shrugged. "I want nuthin' more to do with this so-called doctor. Got me two young'uns, I do. Can't be found floating down the Thames." He turned away.

"Wait..."

But the informant had already disappeared into the night.

There was a crunch of shoes on gravel. A soft splash followed. Then Smith spoke as if to himself, though the information was directed to them. "I'm going to investigate."

Thornton glanced at Black in question. The man shook his head. Because of the malfunctioning device, they'd missed a crucial piece of information.

Rising from behind the boiler, he caught sight of their agent—but not his informant. Smith had climbed into a boat and was rowing down the Thames. Risky, with the Thames' kraken population on the rise. But as long as Smith hugged the shoreline and avoided storm pipes, he might reach his destination—whatever that was—before the smaller kraken swarmed and sank the boat.

But where did that leave them? There was no way to flag down Smith without compromising him. He sagged against the boiler in frustration. At this dark and foggy hour the usual clamor of steam engines, sailors' calls and horns was muted, and through the acousticocept, he could hear the sound of waves lapping at a boat's hull.

So much for simple surveillance.

"There's a dock not far." Black glanced at Thornton's leg. "Can you make it?"

He narrowed his eyes. Such concern was unnecessary. For now. "I can make it."

"Or go down trying," Black retorted.

Before Thornton could snarl an appropriate response, Black was off and running. Using his cane to counterbalance his awkward gait, he followed across the mud and rock of the riverbank, cursing as he stepped on a decaying kraken carcass and nearly lost his footing. The beasts were everywhere, the stench from their decaying bodies rising to fill his nostrils.

By the time he reached said dock, Black was already casting away the ropes. "Hurry up, old man."

Thornton leapt into the boat, and a lightning bolt of pain shot through his leg.

As Black rowed in pursuit and shook free the occasional tentacle that hooked an oar, Thornton unscrewed the silver head of his cane and pulled a glass vial as well as a needle from within. With practiced movements, he fitted the vial with a small needle. Yanking a pant leg above his knee, he injected the contents.

Instant relief. He dragged in a deep breath and shoved the empty vial into his coat pocket.

"Better?" Black asked.

Thornton reassembled his cane and gave a terse nod. As

the tension melted from his muscles, he scanned the water for their man. "There, by the warehouse."

Black adjusted course.

The drug's effectiveness wouldn't last. Once, a single dose had dulled the pain for an entire month. Now he needed to administer the drug daily. It was time to curtail his field duties further. Perhaps eliminate them altogether. Before an agent fell victim to his injury.

A bitter pill to swallow for a man in his early thirties.

In the distance, Smith effortlessly dragged the boat ashore and ducked inside the brick building. His footsteps echoed in Thornton's ear.

"There's a light," the agent whispered. "A faint tapping."

There was a rustle, the sound of a coat being pushed aside and the scrape of a weapon drawn. The agent screamed. An agonizing sound that had both Thornton and Black gripping their ears. An altogether too brief scream that ended with a gurgle. There was a loud crunch followed by telling static.

Though he and Black wore the acousticocept listening devices coiled about their ears, the transmitting device, the acousticotransmitter, had been implanted deep *inside* Smith's ear.

Pulling on the oars, Black beached the boat onto the muddy, trash-laden shore. They ran to the building. Not a single glimmer of light escaped its tall windows. Thornton yanked on the rusty door handle. "Locked."

"Stand back," Black ordered, then kicked the door open, entering with Thornton at his back. Both held their weapons at the ready.

Nothing but silence and their agent, sprawled on the ground—a faint trickle of blood oozing from his ear around a protruding stiletto blade—met their entry.

Thornton clenched his jaw and bent over. He avoided Smith's vacant eyes as he pressed fingers to the agent's throat in the unlikely event that he might find a faint pulse. Nothing. He looked upward, his gaze drawn to the other horror in the room.

Black had flicked on his bioluminescent torch. The cavernous riverside warehouse was filled with stacked wooden crates. In its center, over the delivery hatch in the dock that stretched out over the river, hung a block and tackle. Suspended from the iron hook by rope-bound hands was another man beyond rescue. Blood streaked down his face and neck, soaking the front of a saffron-colored shirt. Empty eye sockets stared down at them.

"Damn it," Black swore. "Not again."

CHAPTER TWO

*T*HE DAY BEGAN MUCH like any other day.

Lady Amanda Ravensdale, daughter of the Duke of Avesbury, took a bite of buttered toast and a sip of cold tea before returning her attention to the femur resting before her on the polished mahogany dining table. A practical examination approached, and she had her heart set on achieving a perfect score. She scanned its surface, murmuring anatomical terms. Greater trochanter, medial epicondyle, linea aspera—

A grinding of gears and a gentle bump against her chair drew her attention. "Thank you, RT," she said to the steambot, lifting a china cup filled with fresh, hot tea. The roving table reversed course and whirred its way back toward the kitchens.

"Must you!" Olivia shrieked from behind her. "The horrors I endure each day as a member of this family. I will never forgive you for caving to such a base desire to mingle with the middle class in an anatomical theater. My sister in medical school. It's a social nightmare."

Amanda smirked at her sister's tantrum and twisted in her chair. "And I will never forgive you for the hours I've lost enduring soliloquy after soliloquy about the difficulties of obtaining an ice sculpture come June."

"I'll have you know planning a proper society wedding is quite an undertaking." Olivia pointed her nose in the air, and golden ringlets bounced about her face. "Carlton will one day be Viscount Bromwich."

"Children," Father warned from the end of the table. He lifted the morning paper higher. On the front page, headlines proclaimed the latest indignity: A German Imperial Fleet zeppelin had attacked what was, the British Navy insisted, a mere merchant's vessel.

"At least a wedding is a suitable pursuit for a lady," Olivia persisted as she stomped over to the buffet. "Carlton says women have no business pursuing a career."

Amanda rolled her eyes. She was thoroughly sick of hearing her future brother-in-law quoted, so she stuck in the proverbial scalpel and gave it a sharp twist. "Carlton simply wants nothing to distract you from your duty as brood mare."

Her sister's jaw unhinged, and she all but dropped her plate of dry toast on the table. "You are so crass. It's to society's benefit that you've set course to become a dried up old maid."

"If that's what it takes to be permitted to use my talents." It wasn't that she opposed marriage. Or children. It was the limitations a husband imposed upon a married female member of the peerage. Not a single man had yet

met her standards. "Though Mr. Sommersby shows promise," she added aloud. He was the only male classmate who
didn't sneer at her presence in the lecture hall. Quite the
opposite. Not that she had *feelings* for him, but she'd
promised Father she would husband hunt.

"The second son of a baron. A mere commoner," Olivia
sniffed, but when she turned toward Father, her expression
grew concerned. "Speaking of marriage and rotten siblings,
any news of Emily?"

Another manifestation of Olivia's obsession with
marrying a title. Scandal might break at any moment.
The *ton* believed Lady Emily visited relatives in Italy, but if
society learned the truth—that their sister had run off with
gypsies to study ancient herbal lore—well, Carlton
wouldn't want anything to do with Olivia.

Worse, Emily had also married Luca, a gypsy she'd
known since childhood—a fact she and Father had kept
from the rest of the family. No need to send Mother and
Olivia into a blind panic. Though Amanda herself was
proud of her sister for taking her future into her own
hands, Father's response was more tempered. He respected
Emily's decision, but had three as-yet unwed children to
manage and a wife who valued her social connections
among the *ton* above all else. As such, all communication
with her sister had been severed.

Father's narrowed eyes appeared over the top of the
paper. "Not a word." He carefully folded the paper, placed
it on the table and pointed to an article. "Though I worry
for her every day."

Amanda leaned forward, reading over her sister's shoulder. There in all its gruesome detail buried at the bottom of page eight:

South London. Another gypsy slain, eyes torn from sockets. One must wonder to what he bore witness.

A small frisson of worry skittered down her spine. Luca's family often settled in South London during the coming winter months, and gypsies traveled in tightly knit family groups. She could only hope that this year his family had chosen another city.

AMANDA STEPPED through the French windows of the library into the crisp, cool autumn air and strolled through the gardens toward the chicken coop. "A good morning to you, Penny," Amanda greeted a fat, white hen.

Penny clucked her usual cheerful response.

Eight years ago, the Town and City Food Act of 1876 had legislated that all homeowners, peers not excepted, contribute to the problem of city-wide food shortages. As duchess, Mother had decreed they would produce eggs rather than put her precious gardens to plow.

Amanda had appropriated the use of the coop's storage room as her laboratory and enlisted the orange-striped cat, Rufus, who now twined about her ankles, as her laboratory assistant. His duties included providing her with mice suffering from spinal injuries, patients obtained during their ill-fated night-time raids on the chicken feed. The cat followed as she moved to a door in the back wall where a lock was mounted. She dialed in a ten-digit security code. Tumblers fell into place and the door swung open.

Potentially useful items cluttered the room. Shelves of glassware, bottles and rubber tubing. Boxes of clockwork components. Stacks of papers and stubs of pencils.

Yet none of the contents mattered save one. On the wide workbench before her, a single cage rested. Inside, a tiny mouse tucked into cotton batting was curled on his side as if in deep sleep. For a brief moment, she held her breath and let herself hope. Perhaps that's all it was, sleep.

She crossed to the bench and bent to examine her patient, watching for the gentle rise and fall of the mouse's ribcage but saw no movement. Still, Amanda clung to hope. Perhaps he breathed shallowly due to the pain of the surgery. That she could ease.

Except there was a smear of blood on the cotton, a clear indication the surgery had failed. Again. Her heart sank.

Rufus leapt beside her and sniffed the mouse through the wire mesh of its cage, performing his own examination. He looked up at her with mournful golden eyes and let out a gut-wrenching yowl.

Dead.

Breakfast congealed into a hard lump in her stomach. She'd had such high expectations last night. Swallowing her disappointment and frustration, Amanda fell back on protocol. She opened the cage, scooping the small, cold mouse from his bedding and slid him into the aethero-scope's observation chamber to seal him from the outside atmosphere. She cranked the handle of the machine, sending concentrated aether though its pipes and valves while activating the vacuum chamber. The device, a birthday present from her brother Ned, replaced oxygen with aether, allowing her to resolve far smaller objects than her other microscope ever had, no matter its powerful objectives.

Perching on a stool, Amanda peered through the eyepiece and twisted the dials into focus. Rotating first one knob and then another, she brought the neuromuscular junction of the muscle into view and sighed. The connection had indeed failed.

Five years ago, after Ned's tragic accident stole the use of his legs, her life-long interest in medicine had found a clear focus. She'd concentrated her efforts on the neuro-muscular system, conceptualizing and then building a neurachnid, a programmable, clockwork spider the size of a bronze halfpence, one that could spin a replacement for a damaged motor neuron following spinal injury.

It sat in a place of honor on a wooden shelf above her workbench. Eight long, hinged legs arched out from a finely mechanized clockwork thorax that controlled the weaving mechanism. Lodged in the abdomen were two other key features. A tiny slot for a miniature Babbage card to direct the neurachnid's activities and a small glass vial, a reservoir for a potent nerve agent administered as the spider worked. The patient's nerve fibers needed to be quieted, but not fully anesthetized, in order for the spider to trace the pathway of the damaged neuron and, using thin gold fibers, reconnect spinal cord to muscle and restore movement.

Last night, the neurachnid had successfully replaced a spinal motor neuron in this mouse. The patient had been able to extend his lower leg. He'd walked for an entire hour. She'd returned her patient to his cage, confident she would find him walking about the cage this morning.

He hadn't. It was still the same problem. The neuro-muscular junction always failed to hold. And when a mouse discovered itself unable to walk, often it reacted by chewing at the fine gold wires, growing increasingly stressed until blood loss and panic simply overwhelmed the tiny creature.

Amanda sat back, punching a button to release the gasses. The microscope hissed and spat, echoing her frustration. She wanted to scream, to fling the spider against the wall and weep for all the hours lost in her futile efforts in this smelly, dim room barely worthy of the term laboratory. She took a deep breath and pushed away the urge.

If only she had a properly equipped laboratory and trained colleagues.

Instead, she picked up the small neurachnid from its shelf and racked her brain looking over the myriad gears and pins, clicks and rivets. If she only could deduce what the problem was, she could devise a solution. But it looked as it always had. She needed fresh eyes. She needed help, competent help that could provide a leap of insight.

She'd tried communicating by post, seeking help from notable neurophysiologists. Most ignored her missives outright, but the handful that responded suggested she abandon her project, citing its impossibility.

But it couldn't be impossible. And she wouldn't quit.

Ned *had* to walk again.

CHAPTER THREE

HORNTON STOOD AT the front of the lecture theater frowning as students filed into the room. The men jostled and shoved, laughing and joking as they crashed about, eventually managing to land in seats. He supposed he'd been much the same as them. Once.

Lister University School of Medicine, founded by the Queen as a co-educational institution to seek out the brightest young medical minds, had not yet managed to find an equal number of women who were capable of passing the rigorous academic exams required for admission. Only three women, all dressed in dark hues, filed into the back row of seats, perching there stiff and solemn, staring down at him intently, like a murder of crows. He distinctly recalled being told there were four women in this class. One of their number was missing.

What had the dean been thinking forcing him to take on this task? Thornton belonged in his laboratory, pressing the boundaries of neuroscience, consulting with the

Queen's agents to stop a murderer who sought to turn Britain's own technology against them. Not stuffing anatomical facts into impenetrable brains.

Ordered by the Queen to the Orkney Islands to investigate a sudden spike in reported sightings of selkies off the coast, Corwin, professor of anatomy, had headed north late last night. The suspicion was that Iceland was dispatching altered Inuit for reasons yet to be determined. Thornton didn't envy the man the dark and cold October nights he would spend perched on the rocky coast. Nevertheless, it meant Professor Corwin required a replacement for the term, and Thornton's physical injuries were no longer considered sufficient excuse for him to avoid teaching obligations.

But lectures were just the start of it all. There would be students in his office asking all manner of questions. Most of them would be ridiculous. Both the questions and the students. So many of them couldn't think their way out of a paper bag. Even worse, there would be exams. Exams he would have to grade. Thornton sighed thinking of the sheer quantity of red ink he would require in the near future. Waste of his time, all of it.

He walked to the podium where the limelight lantern rested, glass projection slides of the human nervous system at the ready. He twisted the gas lines providing both oxygen and hydrogen into "on" positions, picked up the striker and lit the cylinder of quicklime.

There was a lull in the conversation. Thornton cleared his throat and looked up at his audience, expecting all eyes to have focused attentively upon him. Instead, he saw the backs of fifty odd heads and only one face.

A very beautiful face. One with deep pink lips, high cheekbones and a dainty nose between wide eyes that had just a hint of an exotic tilt. Smooth skin, all surrounded by elaborately coiffed hair the color of midnight. Unlike the crows in the back who rolled their eyes in disgust, this woman was garbed in the latest of fashions, a tightly corseted and bustled teal gown with a low cut neckline that had all the men leering.

All but him, of course.

Striking blue eyes met his gaze.

He lifted his eyebrows and drew out his pocket watch to consult the hour. It was five past. She was late.

Her lips curved upward at his obvious reprimand, but she made no effort to hasten her steps. A gentleman in the front row stood, gesturing to a vacant seat he clearly intended for her to occupy. She nodded in greeting, then with the twist of a knob at her waist to collapse her bustle, she removed her feathered hat and settled into the chair beside the smug-looking gentleman.

Instinct told Thornton she would be a problem. A woman with such obvious physical charms expected attention. Best to not provide it. He waved his hand at his assistant and the room plunged into darkness. Sliding home the first glass plate, an illuminated image appeared on the large screen hanging at the front of the hall.

Tomorrow, he would not wait. If she could not manage to arrive promptly, she could damn well stumble her way down the stairs or sit in the back.

"Neurons and glial cells," he intoned. "Later in the laboratory you will closely study the features of both."

~

AMANDA LEANED FORWARD in her chair, entranced by
the deep, booming voice of this new professor. The light
cast by the limelight lantern threw his angular face into
sharp relief. What captivating facial bone structure. Prom-
inent zygomatic arches and a long square jaw made the
planes of his face appear wide and harsh. Between his dark
eyebrows, nasal bones stretched into a long, straight and
distinctive nose. Damp hair severely slicked back from his
forehead betrayed the man by daring to curl at its tips. Full
lips formed words in a tone that made the features of a
neuron sound utterly entrancing.

She rather thought she could be content to spend the
entire morning listening to him read the index of her
anatomy text. Clearly brilliant, he was also the best physical specimen she'd laid eyes on in a long time. Too bad
about that clause in the school's charter forbidding profes-
sors from entering into relationships with their students.

A flush rose upward across her face. Such thoughts. She
forced her gaze to the projection on the screen. *Focus,
Amanda.*

He was proceeding at such a rapid clip that she would soon
be left behind if she could not pull her head out of the aether.

Though she put pen to paper, she could not stop herself
from asking. "What happened to Professor Corwin?" she
whispered to Simon, or Mr. Sommersby as she addressed
him in public.

Simon shifted to lean his shoulder lightly against her
own. Male instinct, she supposed, to mark her as his own.

Behavior she'd encouraged. "No idea. But it seems Lord Thornton is to finish the lecture series."

Her indrawn breath was audible.

Lord Sebastian Talbot, Earl of Thornton and renowned neurophysiologist teaching a course! She'd known he was on staff, but it was rumored that he never lectured. Whatever forced him to the podium, she did not care. Fortune had finally smiled upon her. He might have ignored her attempts to open a scientific correspondence about the possibility of using gold filaments to conduct neurological impulses, but he could not ignore her physical presence in his office as his student.

Excitement must have shown in her face as she contemplated this unexpected windfall, for Lord Thornton's eyes flickered toward her. Did she detect surprise in the slight drawing together of his eyebrows? Hard to be certain, for his words never slowed. She had to convince him of the merit of her work. Convince him to allow her to demonstrate the function of her neurachnid, for his insight would be profound.

He'd already taken notice of her. Twice.

She winced. Not the best first impression. She had been late, and he'd sent quite the scowl in her direction.

If not for the overturned horse cart in the street—horses and steam coaches did not mix well—she would have been punctual. Amanda hated arriving late, enduring the disapproving stares of the other women, the speculative leers of the men. She'd fully intended to politely perch in the back. But when this new professor had met her gaze, seeming to challenge her right to enter, neither fire nor brimstone would have kept her from her usual center seat in the front row.

It was a matter of principle. She'd set a precedent she intended to uphold. Amanda was polite and collegial, stubbornly refusing to be relegated to the dark edges and corners of the room where most male classmates seemed to think she and the other three women belonged.

If only they'd join her.

Betsy, Joan and Sarah clung desperately to the notion that the best manner in which to succeed in medicine as a woman was to efface their sex with severely tailored dresses. Dark colors, long sleeves and high necklines revealing only the oval of their faces. They worked diligently at making themselves unpleasant and uncomfortable. Amanda saw no need to dress the dowd. She took pride in her appearance, and if her ladylike and professional behavior set her apart from others, so be it.

Lord Thornton paced back and forth across the dim lecture hall, a slight hitch to his step, while expounding upon the wonders of the neurological system, changing glass slides with astonishing speed.

Like her classmates, Amanda wrote furiously, her hand cramping. But instead of directing her eyes to the projected images, she stole glances at the man.

With an emphatic wave of his arm, a lock of his hair began to free itself. Another followed. Curls began to assert themselves, twisting tighter and sending waves along each strand. Lord Thornton's hair took on a life of its own, falling across his brow in playful waves.

Though they'd never met, he was *ton* and rumors reached her ears at the various society events she'd been forced to attend. He'd been involved in a terrible dirigible accident, no doubt responsible for the slight limp she detected, but most of the gossip had centered upon his new-found eligibility. For unknown reasons, his long-time fiancée had jilted him mere months before their wedding. Not that any hopeful brides cared why. He was titled and therefore a matrimonial target.

Another slide change. More words rumbled from his throat. His voice was pure intellectual delight. She wrote faster. Really, she must start focusing on the images and not the man. But pressing concerns about the neurachnid's design rose to mind. Here was opportunity. What questions might she put to the great neurophysiologist before her? What flash of brilliant design might she reveal? What was the best path toward winning his regard?

Suddenly, the opportunity was upon her.

The screen went dark, and the room brightened. "If there are no questions," Lord Thornton began. "Tomorrow I will discuss..."

He would send them on their way with no opportunity to engage? She added arrogance to the list of his defining traits. "Professor, with regard to the ganglion, would you consider it possible to transform neurility into electricity via a rare earth metal?"

As intense, blue eyes turned to stare at her, Amanda fancied she'd caught the slightest slackening of his firm, square jaw before it tightened so much his lips thinned. She waited for his answer in breathless anticipation.

"My dear Miss...?" His eyebrows rose in both question and challenge.

"Ravensdale," she supplied. Something in his eyes crystallized, not into ice, but into something much harder and denser, something with razor sharp edges, and she met that piercing gaze with the uneasy sensation in her stomach that things were about to go badly awry.

"Miss Ravensdale. From your... fantastical question, I can only conclude that you have spent far too much time reading texts beyond your comprehension without adequate guidance. Despite their high electrical conductivity, insertion of such elements into the human body would be ethically reprehensible."

Amanda inhaled sharply at the implied reprimand. There were several smothered snickers behind her. Her eyes narrowed as they caught Lord Thornton's gaze. No. She was right and he knew it. With great deliberation, he'd chosen to belittle her hypothesis before her classmates. All hope of a demonstration of her neurachnid followed by his assistance evaporated like a drop of water falling on a hot coal. She pursed her lips, and his eyes flashed with victory.

The arrogant bastard.

Beside her, Simon drew an indignant breath. Amanda pressed her gloved palm to his arm, stifling his impulse to rush to her defense.

Then without further acknowledgement of his audience, Lord Thornton strode from the room.

ABOUT THE AUTHOR

Though ANNE RENWICK holds a Ph.D. in biology and greatly enjoyed tormenting the overburdened undergraduates who were her students, fiction has always been her first love. Today, she writes steampunk romance, placing a new kind of biotech in the hands of mad scientists, proper young ladies and determined villains.

Anne brings an unusual perspective to steampunk. A number of years spent locked inside the bowels of a biological research facility left her permanently altered. In her steampunk world, the Victorian fascination with all things anatomical led to a number of alarming biotechnological advances. Ones that the enemies of Britain would dearly love to possess.

www.annerenwick.com

Printed in the USA
CPSIA information can be obtained
at www.ICGtesting.com
LVHW032229010823
754123LV00040B/623